W9-CDK-165

Stranger
IN THE
Chat Room

Stranger
IN THE
Chat Room

TODD & JEDD
HAFER

BETHANYHOUSE
MINNEAPOLIS, MINNESOTA

Stranger in the Chat Room
Copyright © 2003
Todd and Jedd Hafer

Cover design by Lookout Design Group, Inc.

Scripture quotations are from the HOLY BIBLE, NEW INTERNATIONAL VERSION®. Copyright © 1973, 1978, 1984 by International Bible Society. Used by permission of Zondervan Publishing House. All rights reserved. The "NIV" and "New International Version" trademarks are registered in the United States Patent and Trademark Office by International Bible Society. Use of either trademark requires the permission of International Bible Society.

Material from *In the Chat Room With God* © 2002 by Jedd Hafer and Todd Hafer. Used with permission of Cook Communications Ministries. May not be reproduced further. All rights reserved.

All rights reserved. No part of this publication may be reproduced, stored in a retrieval system, or transmitted in any form or by any means—electronic, mechanical, photo-copying, recording, or otherwise—without the prior written permission of the publisher and the copyright owners.

Published by Bethany House Publishers
11400 Hampshire Avenue South
Bloomington, Minnesota 55438
www.bethanyhouse.com

Bethany House Publishers is a Division of
Baker Book House Company, Grand Rapids, Michigan.

Printed in the United States of America.

Library of Congress CIP Data pending.
Library of Congress Control Number: 2003013805

ISBN 0-7642-2823-4

Finally, be strong in the Lord and in his mighty power. Put on the full armor of God so that you can take your stand against the devil's schemes. For our struggle is not against flesh and blood, but against the rulers, against the authorities, against the powers of this dark world and against the spiritual forces of evil in the heavenly realms. Therefore, put on the full armor of God, so that when the day of evil comes, you may be able to stand your ground, and after you have done everything, to stand. Stand firm then....

Ephesians 6:10–14

Foreword From Tricia Brock of Superchic[k]

I was really honored to be asked to write the foreword for *Stranger in the Chat Room.* I was sent a copy of its predecessor, *In the Chat Room With God,* so I had all these ideas about what this new book was about, and I was so excited to read it. When I finally received *Stranger in the Chat Room,* I just couldn't put it down! I'll be honest; I'm not a huge computer whiz. By the title, I thought maybe it was going to have all this computer lingo and be way over my head! I was completely wrong about that, and I found it was written cleverly, it was really funny, and at the same time really blunt about a lot of issues that so many people are scared to talk about—but let's be honest, they are out there!

Growing up, especially in high school, I was really aware of the presence of evil, tearing away at my friends, lurking around every corner, at every party, whispering to me and my friends, "Just do it....No one will know....You don't even know what you believe....Where is God now?...Why do you feel so lonely?...You're just a loser....Drugs don't really hurt you—it's fun....Why not drink? Everyone else does...." I felt it, I saw the effects, and I saw friend after friend get taken farther and farther away from the truth. Evil is out there. Kids face huge decisions every day; they're tempted and led away from God, from what they were raised believing was true.

I work in a ministry five to seven days out of the week. What we in Superchic[k] hope to do is write music that reaches young people (or maybe just young at heart) because it's honest, it's real. They can relate. We write songs about issues that kids and adults face. We share our own daily struggles in concert. We make ourselves accessible to people. We talk about what we each had to go through to get to God, how faithful He has been to us; that He is everything to us, not just in a little drawer we pull out when it's time to read the Bible every day and then close Him back in and leave Him there.

And we have found that this honesty, this realness that we have with people, is what connects us to them. They open up to us; they share their struggles with us. Not because we're in a band or they think we're cool, but somehow they sense that we really care. Young people are so turned off by people who look down their noses at them because they look different. They want to know they can come to God without outward change, maybe with lots of issues and problems, and that He will take them as they are. They see right through people trying to be "cool" to get their attention.

While reading *Stranger in the Chat Room,* what kept coming to my mind was how real it felt. I didn't feel like I was reading a book written by someone trying to be "hip," trying to impress me with how much they understand youth. Or someone walking on eggshells, afraid to say what they really want to say. I felt like, "The authors understand me, what I've struggled with, and they're meeting me at my level. They want to meet this generation where they are, without the cheesiness and Christianese that sometimes gets used in the process."

I loved the storyline! It held my interest through the very end. I connected with the characters. They are like people I know. I liked that Todd and Jedd weren't afraid to allow the "stranger" in the storyline, to show how easily we let evil in our lives. It reminded me that the spiritual realm is close, that I have to know who I'm serving every day. Evil is out there, always ready to devour, but we can be sure that when we belong to God, our side will win!

The conversations between the Lord and the characters in the book make it feel so evident that He wants a relationship with us. He wants to be our friend, to be our Protector, to be our Father, to be so much more than we let Him be. I really enjoyed *Stranger in the Chat Room,* and I'm sure you will too! If you're young (or not so young, just young at heart), and you're thinking about getting this book—go for it! I hope you enjoy it as much as I did!

Contents

A Few Words About Stranger in the Chat Room

The final score was 143 to 92. Evil defeated Good.

And, no, this isn't the score of some bizarre fantasy basketball game. It's taken directly from the Bible. While creating this book, we flipped to the concordance of our research Bible and compared the number of references to "evil" or "evildoers" to the number of times the word "good" appears (when it's used in the sense of a virtue). Evil won by a substantial margin.

Why? we wondered.

Why would God allow evil to outnumber good in His holy Book? The answer became clear after we turned from the concordance to some actual Scripture text. In Ephesians 6, Paul notes that Christians are in a struggle, a battle. And that battle pits us against "spiritual forces of evil."

Our old football coach, Coach Corky, used to say, "Ya gots to know your enemy if'n ya wants to win." Corky wasn't much of a grammarian, but he understood the nature of a battle, whether it's played out on a rectangular acre of green grass or in the hearts, minds, and souls of human beings.

God knows we are at war. That's why He devoted so much space in His Word to our enemy. He wants us to understand the evil we battle, and He wants to equip us with the armor and weapons necessary to win.

The teen characters in this book confront a diabolical evildoer. Some are well-equipped for battle; others aren't. Further, in the heat of a struggle, some of them make wise, brave choices; others do not. In the spirit of honesty, we are compelled to present it all.

We've absorbed criticism for portraying evil realistically in this book. That's OK with us. We believe that if God wasn't afraid to address evil in His Book, then we shouldn't be either.

It's in that spirit, and in the spirit of C. S. Lewis, that we created *Stranger in the Chat Room.* (Lewis's writing has always been one of our spiritual staples.) Lewis's classic *The Screwtape Letters* has profoundly affected our lives. In *Screwtape,* Lewis reveals possible motives and methods behind the hell-born temptation every Christian will face. Yes, it's unpleasant to think that there is a schemer out there, plotting our downfall, but should we ignore that fact? If we do, we have already succumbed to defeat.

Ephesians 6:13–14 commands us to "stand firm," to stand our ground. The genius and courage of Lewis have helped many Christians to better understand just what—and whom—we stand against.

So we've stood on the shoulders of a giant and found the view rather frightening. Still, we must be honest about what we see. For only when we truly understand an enemy can we defeat him decisively and finally. We have our old coach's word on that. More important, we have our Heavenly Father's word on it.

We are grateful for the opportunity to share this book with you. We hope and pray it can serve to carry on the message that Mr. Lewis first published more than forty years ago. We owe thanks to C. S. Lewis for his pioneering work. And we are also grateful to the many teens who candidly shared with us their struggles, their emotions, their opinions, and their faith.

So to the teens at Wasson High School, Doherty High School, Woodland Park High School, Monticello Trails Middle School, Southwoods Christian Church, Colorado Springs Christian School, Pulpit Rock Church, and The Children's Ark, thank you. This book wouldn't exist without you.

By the way, if that Good-versus-Evil score is still troubling you, consider this: In that same biblical concordance, "love"—and cousins like "loving-kindness" and "loving"—appears 754 times, more than Good and Evil combined. We think God did that on purpose—to assure us that, no matter who the opponent or how fierce the battle, love conquers all.

A Note About the Net

The fictitious teens in this book find friendship and support on the Internet. They also find evil. We hope that this latter aspect can serve as a cautionary tale to our readers. In today's virtual world, teens are likely to find pornography, scam artists, predators, tempters, and liars. During our years researching this book, we met some delightful people on the Net; we also met many who were dishonest, profane, hostile, and deeply disturbed. We read recently about a police officer who was part of an Internet sting operation. Posing as a young teenage boy, he encountered an adult who wanted to meet him in person. A meeting was arranged. An Internet predator was arrested. In this case, the culprit was a coach who thought he was meeting a thirteen-year-old boy.

If you have found trustworthy friends on the Net, that's cool. If you're a person of faith, perhaps you have found soul mates who can relate to your spirituality. That's even better than cool. However, we urge you to spend time in God's Word and to relate to authentic, flesh-and-blood, trustworthy people. The virtual world can be more dangerous than it is useful.

With these thoughts in mind, please heed the following caveats as you surf, chat, instant-message, create online profiles, etc.:

- Don't give anyone your Internet password.
- Don't think there are exceptions to the above warning. There aren't.
- Be extremely careful about giving anyone your scanned photo, phone number, or home address.
- Keep track of information your chat buddies give about themselves, and check them periodically. For example, if you ask someone his or her age one day, wait a few days, then ask for a birthdate. (And this answer should come quickly; this isn't the kind of answer that involves

multivariable calculus.) Compare answers. If you are being lied to, end the relationship and block that person's attempts to contact you.

- Unless it's in the context of a church/community youth group or school event, don't agree to meet an Internet pal in person. (If you have become friends with someone over a *long* period of time and feel a face-to-face meeting is warranted, discuss it with a parent or trusted adult first. Don't go alone to meet someone. Do meet in a safe public place—a hotel doesn't qualify.)

- Don't waste your time and talent spending too many hours online. The Net is an intriguing place, but it's no substitute for an actual life. If you insist on obsessing over all things Internet, read a nice book about it. This one, for example.

In short, we see nothing inherently wrong with spending a reasonable amount of time exploring the World Wide Web. Just don't get tangled up in it.

Prologue: The Back Story

This book features characters introduced in our book *In the Chat Room With God*. However, it's not a pure sequel. You don't have to read *In the Chat Room With God* to appreciate *Stranger in the Chat Room*. (Although we won't object if you decide to get both books.)

Just in case you're now wondering what happened in the first book, here's a summary:

CrossKrys, a skeptic about the existence of God, and JennSmiles, an angry cynic on the subject, meet accidentally one night while searching for guys in a public chat room called Romantic Rendezvous.

Later, they encounter Blake7, a self-avowed Jesus Freak who challenges their doubts, listens to their concerns, and prays for their souls. The trio begins a series of private chats, in a series of rooms named for the theme of a particular evening's topic. One night, as the trio debates the existence of God, someone claiming to be the Supreme Being himself invades a private chat session. At first, the girls accuse Blake of orchestrating this "divine" appearance, but gradually they begin to sense that this mysterious Visitor possesses heavenly wisdom, love, and power.

Even Jenn's drug-addled tagalong friend, A.C.008, is intrigued as this *being* claiming to be God leads them on a journey in which hard questions are posed and answered, emotions are laid bare, tragic secrets are revealed, and grace flows like a pure, healing river.

Over the course of a school year, Blake's faith is strengthened, and Krys and Jenn, for the first time in their lives, encounter the power of God's saving love. A.C., unfortunately, drops out of the group, deciding he'll win—or lose—his battle against addiction on his own.

At the end of the school year, God informs the group that He will be leaving the chat sessions—but He assures everyone, "You will always be able to find me." Meanwhile, Blake departs on a cross-country bike trip. Krys leaves her home state (Wyoming) to spend the summer with her biological mother (who doesn't own a computer) in Montana. Blake introduces his friends to his little sister, Lorri, who scoffs at the existence of God and harbors deep resentment toward her "too-perfect" big brother.

Jenn attempts to strike up a friendship with Lorri—a friendship that doesn't appear too promising, at first.

To learn even more about the characters that populate *Stranger in the Chat Room,* check out Appendix A, which features online-style profiles of Krys, Jenn, Lorri, Blake, and A.C. And while you're back there in Appendix Land, you can read Appendix B, which features the final three chapters from *In the Chat Room With God.* (Our thanks to RiverOak Publishing and Cook Communications for letting us reprint those chapters.) If you're really into the whole appendix thing, you can also find a glossary of Internet slang and teen-tested and teen-approved contemporary slang.

OK, then, enough of this prefatory stuff. On to the first chapter—there's a private chat going on, and you're welcome to eavesdrop....

The adventure begins here....

PRIVATE CHAT #120

Where Do We Go From Here?

 PARTICIPANTS HERE: 2
Strider77 • JennSmiles

JENNSMILES: This is weird.

STRIDER77: What is weird?

JENNSMILES: Being back to normal again. No Supreme Deity in the chat room. I thought He would show up from time to time, but it's been a month and a half. I've got a feeling He's done with the chat-room thing. But I miss Him.

STRIDER77: Really? Be honest with me.

JENNSMILES: I'm telling you straight up. Once I was convinced that the mysterious invader was God, it made me feel special that He would take the time to talk to ME.

STRIDER77: OK, let me play devil's advocate, if you'll pardon the expression.

JENNSMILES: Advocate away.

STRIDER77: You said it made you feel special when this person you believe to be God visited your chats. But good old big brother Blake is always going off about how God has tried to communicate with humanity through the ages. Writing on tablets of stone. Speaking from a cloud—or even a burning bush. Sending prophet after prophet. Inspiring the Bible. It would seem to me that if there is a God, he's done a heck of a lot to communicate with needy chicks like you.

JENNSMILES: He has.

STRIDER77: But you didn't feel special until he visited your chat. What about all the other stuff? Why didn't any of that make you feel special?

JENNSMILES: Good point.

STRIDER77: I don't want to make a point. I want an answer.

JennSmiles: I don't know. I guess I didn't see how all that other stuff related to me. But now I kinda do.

Strider77: Huh?

JennSmiles: The Bible is different to me now. Before, I saw most of it as boring history, or pseudo-history. Some of it was irrelevant. And the rest was a bunch of rules that I didn't want to obey. But now I see how it guides me. How it assures me. How it reveals this God who is so complex but pretty darn simple at the same time. When you boil it all down, here's what's left: It's all about love, baby.

Strider77: You sound like Blake.

JennSmiles: Thanks. That's a compliment.

Strider77: Not from where I'm sitting. Don't get me wrong. He's nice to me. But too nice. He suffocates me. Besides, I don't see how someone as smart as he is can believe in fairy tales. And I hate people assuming that I'm a Christian like he is. If I get called Sister Lorri one more time, I'm leavin' a Reebok footprint on somebody's face.

JennSmiles: Do you think Blake loves you?

Strider77: Do you want me to puke?

JennSmiles: What's wrong, Stride? You can talk tough, but can you be honest? Anyone can pose like a real hard-head. Half the guys in my school acted all ghetto. But it was mostly smoke and mirrors. And, listen to this, anti-Sister Lorri, it's a lot harder to give an honest answer than it is to just give attitude.

Strider77: I don't know....

JennSmiles: I do. I have found that most of the world is afraid to be real. I was. I reinvented myself more times than Madonna. But no more. And I have Blake to thank for that. Blake and, uh, You Know Who.

Strider77: This is boring me. I think I'm gonna bounce.

JENNSMILES: I don't think it's boring you. I think it's making you uncomfortable. It's givin' you a soul itch. I think you don't want to admit Blake loves you. Or that God loves you. And I think I'm scaring you.

STRIDER77: Hey, wo-man, nothing scares me!

JENNSMILES: I think plenty scares you. I think you're scared to consider the real world. I think you're afraid to consider what might lie beyond your cozy little Disney World o' Denial. Come on, Stride. Don't you ever lie in bed and think about why you're here—and what will happen to you after you're gone? Don't you ever think about death and contemplate eternity: What happens to a person in those long, last moments between life and death? Is it a time of terror or peace? Or is all of this just too deep for you? Too powerful for you to deal with?

STRIDER77: You know, I've had a gut-full of you. I'm out.

JENNSMILES: Go ahead and run. Blake said you are good at running. I just didn't know he meant running AWAY.

STRIDER77: Whatever. Bye.

JENNSMILES: Let's say until next time.

STRIDER77: What makes you think there will be a next time?

JENNSMILES: Because you and I are going to be friends. I have a feeling.

STRIDER77: I don't feel anything.

JENNSMILES: Maybe that's your problem. Anyway, Ms. Lorri, I like you. Let's connect again.

STRIDER77: Doubtful.

JENNSMILES: Maybe not. As I said before, I think you've got a soul itch, and who else is gonna scratch it for you?

STRIDER77: What in the world is a soul itch?

JENNSMILES: Maybe I'll tell you next time we talk. I'm signing off now. Love ya, Stride.

Private Chat #121

I'm Baaaaack!

PARTICIPANTS HERE: 2
JennSmiles • Strider77

STRIDER77: I'm here, but don't gloat. Or I'll leave.

JENNSMILES: No gloating here. I'm just grateful that you are here.

STRIDER77: Woman, puh-leeze!

JENNSMILES: It's true.

STRIDER77: Jenn, can we get something straight between us?

JENNSMILES: Shoot.

STRIDER77: I am not your project, OK? I would like to be your friend. But I don't want or need a spiritual mentor or whatever. If that's all I am to you, your spiritual craft project, it's over.

I get enough of that from Blake. And I can't disown my brother, unfortunately. Some Rocky Mountain cyber-chick, that's another story.

JennSmiles: Stride—I'm your friend. No matter what. You can be president of the Young Atheists of America, and we'll still be friends. Just don't try to sell me any cookies, magazine subscriptions, or whatever the Young Atheists are peddling these days.

Strider77: Well, we can bet it's not angel food cake.

JennSmiles: A joke? From a blood relative of Blake Randall?

Strider77: Yeah, I got the sense of humor in the family. And the looks too.

JennSmiles: You don't say? You know, I never could get Blake to send me a pic. He wouldn't even describe himself. So you're my source. So tell me.

STRIDER77: Is it your mission in life to make me blow my groceries? You want me to tell you that my brother is *hot*?

JENNSMILES: Well? Is he? Is he hot? Is he cut? Do distance runners lift weights or what?

STRIDER77: He is...I don't know...OK, I guess. I never really thought of him in a hot/not-hot sorta way, until now. Thank you so much for tainting the last remaining pure element of my childhood.

JENNSMILES: I'm sorry. But I have asked God to take away my sins, not my hormones. C'mon, you can't blame me for being curious, can you?

STRIDER77: Oh, I don't know. Can we PLEASE change the subject? I'll even talk about God if we can get off of this particular topic.

JENNSMILES: Deal. Hey, hang on—I just got an IM. Oh my goodness! Stride, I am so amped! I think it's Krys. She must have made a computer-owning friend in Montana!

WATCHER55: Hey, my friends!

JENNSMILES: Krys? Is it really you? What's with the screen name—why not use your own?

WATCHER55: It's my new bud's moniker. He's letting me have some screen time before he checks his email.

JENNSMILES: HE? You already snagged a guy?

WATCHER55: No, it is nothing like that. We're talking pure platonic friendship here.

STRIDER77: That's what they all say.

WATCHER55: Ah, the punk kid sister speaks. So, Lorri, have you caved in and converted yet? Followed the big brother up the narrow staircase that leads to heaven?

STRIDER77: Uh, no.

JENNSMILES: Whoa, Krys. What's with the harsh?

WATCHER55: *What's with the harsh?* You know, Jenn, the more you try to sound cool, the more you end up sounding pathetic. What's with the inability to communicate like an intelligent adult? Like, why are you, like, so, ya know, whateverish?

JennSmiles: Well, I'm not an adult yet. And I haven't mastered the art of eloquent adultspeak. I promise to sign up for Toastmasters ASAP. But even though I am just an ignorant teen, I know my friends, especially my best friend. And you, Watcher55, are not Krys. So if this is a joke, it sucks. Now, if Krys is there, let HER talk to me. If not, you know what you can do.

Strider77: OK, this is too trippy. What is going on?

Watcher55: <sigh> What is going on is just a joke gone bad. Girls, I apologize. I've acted poorly. Krys is downstairs. She'll be up soon. She told me I could try to hook up with you two while she got us a couple of Diet Cokes. My name is Haddon. I'm nineteen. I have lived in Montana all of my life. I do some yard work for Krys's mom. That's how we met. Once she heard I had a computer, we became fast friends.

STRIDER77: Oh...

JENNSMILES: I see. So, Haddon, is Krys upstairs with those Diets yet? So the two of you can quench your respective thirsts?

WATCHER55: Not yet. But I hope she hurries. I'm parched.

JENNSMILES: No, what you are, actually, is busted.

WATCHER55: Huh?

STRIDER77: Let me second that: "Huh?"

JENNSMILES: Stride, log off right now, OK? We will connect later.

STRIDER77: OK, can someone tell me what's going on? I'm not loggin' off until I know what's the what here.

JENNSMILES: OK. Quick explanation and then you bounce, Stride. This guy is lying. You didn't do your research,

Haddon. You and Krys aren't going to be slurping down Diet Cokes together. She wouldn't drink diet if you held a gun to her head. She is a one-woman crusade against artificial sweeteners. She tried to make me promise her I'd never drink another diet anything. Besides, the only time I heard a teen guy use a word like "parched" was in our high-school production of *Oklahoma*. So you, my nonfriend, are a lying sack. Stride, we're out of here now, OK? I'll report this mook to the ISP later. Bye-bye, Haddon, it's been a real puke-fest to meet ya.

STRIDER77: Yeah, what she said. We out.

WATCHER55: :' (

WATCHER55: Ah, the girls are gone. Good-bye, girls. But we'll chat again soon. You won't be able to refuse me. We are going to become soooo close this summer. I can feel it. And the things I will get you to do! You will be shocked and amazed. And changed forever.

You might be afraid of me at first, but there is really nothing to fear. All I want is to mess with your heads a bit. Maybe mess with your souls, too. But what I really want is that freak Blake. I want his soul most of all. And not just to mess with it—to devour it. To destroy it forever.

Private Chat #122

Reunited

 PARTICIPANTS HERE: 2
JennSmiles • Blake7

JENNSMILES: B, is it really you?

BLAKE7: Yes, in the virtual flesh. I'm using my roommate's laptop.

JENNSMILES: It is so cool to hear from you. Hey, how is the big ride going?

BLAKE7: It's great. Some days I think I'll need the Jaws of Life to extract me from my bike saddle, but I'm getting in shape. How's your summer so far?

JENNSMILES: Passing by too quickly. I'm working a little. Tanning a lot. Trying to decide what to do with my life.

BLAKE7: Still going to youth group?

JennSmiles: Wow—it took a whole fifty-two seconds before you asked the inevitable question! Yes, B, I am still going. It's not easy. I feel out of place most of the time. But I'm trying. I'm trying really hard.

Blake7: Keep at it. You'll feel more comfortable in time. Just don't get too comfortable.

JennSmiles: Huh? What do you mean?

Blake7: A youth group needs someone to ask the hard questions, to bring a fresh perspective. To shake things up a bit. And I know you're a person who can shake it!

JennSmiles: So you're actually encouraging me to be a non-conformist?

Blake7: In a way I am. Jesus came to save individuals, one at a time, not by committees or groups. Sometimes people get in a group and they start to think alike, act alike. They go on autopilot. They go brain-dead. You get in there and mix it up, Jenn. Keep things alive.

JENNSMILES: You know me, Blake. I can't do it any other way.

BLAKE7: Jenn, I can't tell you how thrilled I am that you're still on the Way.

JENNSMILES: Sure you can. You just did.

BLAKE7: I guess I did, at that. I'm sorry if I'm on happiness overkill here. But I'm just so relieved. I worry about you.

JENNSMILES: Well, thanks. But you really shouldn't worry about me. I'm in good hands. Bigger hands than yours, even. It's your sister who worries me. We've been talking a lot, B. And please don't get upset at me for saying this, but the girl is messed up. She has issues.

BLAKE7: Yeah, she's going through kind of a cynical phase right now. Especially about God and stuff. She'll grow out of it eventually.

JENNSMILES: Hmmm.

BLAKE7: I don't like the look of that "Hmmm." What's up?

JENNSMILES: Just this: Why is every crisis a teen goes through called a "phase"— something she'll grow out of or pass through, like a car wash or something? "Just put your life in neutral and sit back, baby. It's going to get dark and scary and noisy now, but in a little while you'll pop out the other side, clean and sparkling new. Then you'll be ready to drive on to that lovely place called The Rest of Your Life!"

BLAKE7: I'm not sure I get your point.

JENNSMILES: Oh, give me a large, personal break! Blake, stick with me here: How old does Lorri—or any teen, for that matter—have to be before her problems get to be real? If a forty-year-old woman went to her shrink or pastor and said, "My life lacks direction, and I'm unsure about the very existence of God," would she get told, "Just hang in there, sweetie. By the time you're forty-five, everything will work out; everything will make sense. And your acne will clear up too!"

BLAKE7: C'mon, Jenn…

JENNSMILES: No, why don't you c'mon—off your perch so that you can get down on your sister's level. What she's going through RIGHT NOW matters, Blake! Her problems are real. Teens kill themselves every day over problems like Lorri's. If it's really just a phase, how come so many people don't come out of it alive? Tell me why, please?!

BLAKE7: Jenn, I'm...I don't know.

JENNSMILES: Spit it out: You're _____ . What? Sorry, confused, ashamed?

BLAKE7: All of the above. And busted as well. I was just rereading what you said. And you know what? You're right. I've been condescending to Lorri, for the past two years at least. No wonder she hates me. I've treated her like an immature kid.

JENNSMILES: Which she is in a lot of ways. But her problems are real. They hurt. And if they matter to your sister, they should matter to you too. Think about it—she's trying to figure out who God is and what that means for her life. That's a big deal. Whether you're thirteen or thirty-one.

BLAKE7: I feel so guilty.

JENNSMILES: You should.

BLAKE7: I've tried so hard to set a good example for her. I watch my language. I don't watch certain TV shows. I make sure I study my Bible in the living room, where she can see me. I pray before every meal. I don't miss church or youth group, even when I'm sick. I'm disciplined in school and in my sports. I'm disciplined in everything, really.

JENNSMILES: Oh, well, big ups to Mr. Blake Randall, Super Christian! Gosh, can I feel your muscles? You're quite the teen achiever, aren't you?

BLAKE7: Don't come at me like that, Jenn. I'm not trying to brag. I'm just trying to show you how hard I work to model good behavior for my little sister.

JENNSMILES: "Model good behavior"? Who do you think you are, Dr. Phil? You know, maybe you should leave the modeling to Gisele, Tyra, and Frederique.

BLAKE7: But…but…

JENNSMILES: Blake, get your "buts" out of here. Listen to me: You need to stop trying so hard to be Mr. Perfect Role Model. Maybe you should just focus on being Lorri's brother. That's what she needs. I know she's so smart that she skipped a grade. But thirteen and a half is thirteen and a half, no matter what your IQ is.

BLAKE7: OK, Jenn. I will do that; I promise. Wow. When did you get so wise?

JENNSMILES: I didn't mean to blow ya mind, B. And I appreciate the compliment, but understanding people really isn't a matter of smarts. All you have to do is listen, really listen. Sometimes Lorri and I will be online, or on the phone, and she'll get into this long rant, and I won't say a word. I just listen to what she's saying and how she's saying it. Don't get me wrong; it's cool to be helped. But it's cool just to be heard too. And I think you have to truly listen to people before you can help them.

BLAKE7: You're right, Jenn. Thanks so much for having my sister's back.

JENNSMILES: It's what friends do.

BLAKE7: Speaking of friends, have you heard from Krys?

JENNSMILES: We've phoned a few times. But her Biological Mom still doesn't have a computer. Can you believe that? What—do people still live in caves up in Montana? I told her just last week, "K, you gotta get connected. Make some friends whose 'rents actually own a computer. Find a dude with a Dell or something!" B, I miss her so much. Her Bio Mom will let us talk only once a week, max.

BLAKE7: Maybe she'll get hooked up soon. You know Krys. She's resourceful. Hey, Kirk is here and he needs to check his emails, so I gotta go. But, real quick, have you heard from Ace?

JennSmiles: Nada. I don't even know if he's still alive. Maybe he OD'd or something. Let's keep praying for him.

Blake7: Will do.

JennSmiles: Me too. And, B, look for me next time you're online. I need your help with this weird guy that hacked into a private chat with Lorri and me last week.

Blake7: Maybe it's just one of Lorri's friends pranking you. She rolls with a strange crowd. Or maybe it was Ace. Have you thought about that?

JennSmiles: I don't know....

Blake7: Look, Jenn, I'm so sorry but I gotta sign off. Google this intruder by his screen name. Maybe you'll turn up something. We'll talk later. I'm out.

JennSmiles: OK. Good-bye. Peace-out, B.

Watcher55: Ah, I love tender good-byes.

JennSmiles: Whatever, freak. How do you feel about harsh good-byes, 'cuz that's what you're about to experience. I don't know how you got in one of my rooms again, but I'm sure you can find your way out!

WATCHER55: Why take your anger out on me, Jennifer? Blake is the one who dissed you. You mentioned this evil genius who hacked his way into your private chat with his beloved little sister, and what did he do? He bolted from this chat room like it was on fire. Luckily, I'm still here for you.

JENNSMILES: First, I never said you were a genius. Second, I don't need you anywhere for me, except gone. More specifically, how do you feel about hell? Perhaps you could go there—know what I'm sayin'?

WATCHER55: Hell, eh? Do you believe in hell, Jennifer? Do you have any idea about the place you've just tried to banish me to? Or is it a place? Maybe it's just a state of mind. Maybe, if we focus our minds, we can take a peek into hell right now! Whaddya say?

JENNSMILES: OK, you're creeping me out. Would you PLEASE just leave me alone?!

WATCHER55: You don't need to fear me, Jennifer. I'm not here to hurt you. I just want to talk with you.

JENNSMILES: Well, that makes ONE of us. And the other one is out. Buh-bye.

WATCHER55: C'mon, my friend. Don't go. We have much to talk about. Much to share.

JENNSMILES: OK, which part of what I just said DIDN'T you understand—the "buh" or the "bye"? I'm signing off. Now.

WATCHER55: Ah, gone again. Good-bye, my friend. You'll be back soon. You can't resist me. This is all working out quite well, just the way we planned it.

Secret Session #1

PARTICIPANTS HERE: 2
Watcher55 • Ghost9

WATCHER55: So are we having fun yet?

GHOST9: Fun isn't the objective here. Remember that.

WATCHER55: Well, it's fun for some of us.

GHOST9: Whatever melts your cheese, Haddon. You just stay focused. You have a job to do. Just do it. Then we can all get on with our lives.

WATCHER55: I never lose my focus, Ghost. You'll learn that about me as we get to know each other better. You will be pleased with my results.

GHOST9: I hope so. I just don't see things coming together very fast. I want this done by the end of the summer, remember.

WATCHER55: It will be done on schedule. We still have much time. Have some patience.

GHOST9: I'm not exactly known for my patience. And remember, if I don't get what I want, you don't get what you want.

WATCHER55: I know. I know. But you must know that it will take some time to do this right. On that topic, thanks for the great intel on Krys! She's this huge crusader against artificial sweeteners, and you didn't know about it? You blew my cover way too early, Ghost. You got sloppy.

GHOST9: Hey, I can't know everything. I did the best I could. Let's not get carried away with the whole espionage thing, OK? You're not James Bond, remember. Dude, why don't I get you a ladder so you can climb off my back now?

WATCHER55: Calm down, Ghost. It's OK. I'm just pointing out that if you want me to forgive your errors, you must allow me the time to do this mission right. You must be patient. And you must provide me thorough and accurate intel.

GHOST9: OK, I'll try, Agent Double-Zero. But if you don't make something happen soon, I'm squashing this whole deal.

WATCHER55: Just watch and enjoy, Ghost. I think you'll be quite pleased by the time we have our next clandestine session. Two weeks from tonight. See you then.

GHOST9: Don't be late.

WATCHER55: Ha ha ha ha ha ha ha ha. I'm never late.

Private Chat #123

Are We Safe?

 PARTICIPANTS HERE: 3
JennSmiles • Strider77 • Watcher55

JENNSMILES: Let's see: To paraphrase *Sesame Street:* "One of these peeps is not like the others / One of these peeps just doesn't belong."

STRIDER77: Or is it "one of these CREEPS"?

WATCHER55: Hmmm, I wonder whom you could be talking about.... You've named this chat room Are We Safe? Do you mean safe from me? Do I frighten you?

JENNSMILES: Yeah, you're so annoying that it's scary. Look, you are not welcome here. And I'm going to report you if you don't stop harassing us.

WATCHER55: Last month you said you were going to report me, but you didn't.

You are obviously very perceptive. You know there's no need to involve the cyber-police. You know in your heart that I'm not out to hurt you, Jennifer. You either, Strider. I have just, by chance, happened to cross virtual paths with two charming, fascinating young women. I've enjoyed our conversations. Even when you've become angry with me. I'm learning a lot.

STRIDER77: But why can't you learn to tell when you're not wanted? Please, just leave us alone.

WATCHER55: Why are you so afraid of me, Lorri? Look at what we're doing— just typing words on computer screens. You're not afraid of a few words, are you?

STRIDER77: You don't scare me. Don't flatter yourself.

JENNSMILES: Yeah, we're not afraid. Nauseated is more like it. You, my not-friend, are puke-worthy.

WATCHER55: You hardly know me, Jennifer. How could you make a harsh judgment like that?

JENNSMILES: It's easy: "Hey, Watcher, you make me wanna blow chow!"

WATCHER55: I'm hurt. And confused by your animosity. I've done nothing that should have an emetic effect on you. I don't use profanity. I don't tell coarse jokes. I don't make sexual advances. I'm just an honest individual trying to have an intelligent, meaningful conversation with two young women whom I find intriguing.

JENNSMILES: I'd like to know how you found us in the first place.

WATCHER55: Who said I found you? Perhaps we found each other. Perhaps it was fate.

JENNSMILES: WONNNNNK! (That's my game-show buzzer sound, in case you didn't know.) Wrong answer, Mr. Watcher. Thanks for playing. We have some nice parting gifts for you. Pick up your year's supply of Turtle Wax at the door as you exit from our lives!

WATCHER55: See what I mean? You are charming indeed. And funny too.

JENNSMILES: I see what you're trying to do, Haddon—that's what you said your real name was, remember? (I'm sure it's not your real name, but I'm throwin' you a bone so that you can at least lie with some consistency.) Anyway, you're trying to flatter us. But it isn't going to work. We see the truth: You're some pathetic mook stalker who can't seem to accept the fact that we don't enjoy your company. And listen to me, I didn't report you before because… well, I don't know why. But that doesn't mean I won't. Got it?

WATCHER55: Got it. And thank you for calling me Haddon. That's a sign that our relationship is growing. It is my real name, by the way.

JENNSMILES: Yeah. I'm sure it is. OK, WATCHER! You're totally creeping us out here. Don't you have any other girls you can go play *American Psycho* with?

STRIDER77: For real, Watcher. Enough is enough.

WATCHER55: OK. How about I make you a deal?

JENNSMILES: If the deal involves you disappearing forever, I'm listening.

WATCHER55: I'm game for that.

STRIDER77: So let's hear it.

WATCHER55: Jennifer, I understand you believe in God?

JENNSMILES: You understand correctly. But how did you know that?

WATCHER55: It's quite obvious, actually, to the perceptive observer. Anyway, the whole God thing, it's important in your life, correct?

JENNSMILES: Not "it." He. God is a personal being, not a thing. He is important in my life.

WATCHER55: Very well, then. Has it—I mean HE—made your life better?

JennSmiles: Uh, yeah—in the sense that He SAVED my life, you moron.

Watcher55: Really? So your life is now better in every way? Tell the truth. You know what they say, "The truth will set you free."

JennSmiles: "They" didn't say that. Jesus did. And to answer your question, I think my life is better in every way. It's harder in some respects, but it's still better. I care more—about people, about life in general. And life is harder when you care, but I don't want to go back to the way I was.

Watcher55: I'm glad you brought up caring. You Christians, you're supposed to care for others, right?

JennSmiles: Duh, Einstein.

Watcher55: So if you truly care for other people, and you have something that has enhanced your life...

JennSmiles: Not something. Someone.

WATCHER55: Point taken. But I'm still confused here. This someone has enhanced your life, and one would think you would want to share your experience with the lost world out there. But I get the sense that you haven't done that, have you, Jennifer?

JENNSMILES: I guess you are right. I have tried to talk to Lorri, but I haven't made much headway there, right, Strider?

STRIDER77: Whatever. Can we just leave me out of this?

WATCHER55: Good suggestion, "Strider." Let's get back to you, Jennifer. If God has transformed your life, why are you keeping it to yourself? You're a failure, as far as I'm concerned. Doesn't the Bible say something about going to all nations and preaching the Good News? Or do you think that "keep the faith" means "keep it to yourself"?

JENNSMILES: Maybe you're right. Maybe I have failed so far. But I'm not a missionary, you know. I am new to this. I'm still learning the ropes.

WATCHER55: So by your line of reasoning, if you were a novice cook, you wouldn't prepare food for starving people because what you cooked wouldn't meet gourmet standards?

JENNSMILES: I didn't say that. I wouldn't let people starve if I had the power to help them.

STRIDER77: Yeah, you're twisting her words!

WATCHER55: I'm merely taking her pathetic excuse down the path to its logical conclusion.

JENNSMILES: You know what—why don't you take the path to the end of the world! And when you get there, take a flying leap! I'm not a selfish person! I'm a giving person! Ask anybody who knows me.

WATCHER55: Jennifer, Jennifer, Jennifer. You're losing focus. We were about to make a deal that could remove me from your life forever, and my, oh my: You've become sidetracked. You've lost your way.

JennSmiles: Whatever, freak. And I didn't forget about the deal. Let's hear it.

Watcher55: Well, before you went off on that tangent, we were talking about your failure to share your belief in God. You were trying to justify your selfish stance. I, on the other hand, was trying to encourage you to be more generous with this great gift of faith.

JennSmiles: And? I'm losing patience here! Can you get to the point? 'Cuz right now I'd do just about anything to get rid of you.

Strider77: Yeah! Get to the point or get lost.

Watcher55: Very well, then. Jennifer, I'll give you one week. All you have to do is share your faith with one non-believing person—and get that person to pray with you.

JennSmiles: Are you for real?

Watcher55: I'm very real. You can read, can't you? You're so amped about God? Tell somebody about him if you really believe he is real. Face-to-face. It can be a total stranger or one of your non-believing friends, assuming any of them ARE still your friends.

JennSmiles: Bite me!

Watcher55: Ah, hit a nerve, did I? The truth does hurt, doesn't it?

Strider77: Hey, Haddon, leave her alone, OK? And by the way, I'M her friend. And so is Krys.

Watcher55: Yes, Krys. I'd like to meet her someday.

JennSmiles: You claimed you already did meet her, remember, you lying sack?! And I wish she was here right now. She's whip-smart, and she'd carve you up like a Thanksgiving turkey.

Watcher55: Perhaps we'll see about that someday. But now to the challenge at hand: How about it, Jennifer? One conversation about God. One little prayer meeting with one of God's precious lost lambs—your target doesn't even need to pray for salvation. Just pray to God about anything. You pull that off, and I'm gone from your lives forever.

JennSmiles: Well, I like the sound of that.

Watcher55: I know you do. And to make things even more interesting, if you meet the challenge, I'll send you one thousand dollars, in cash.

JennSmiles: Yeah, sure you will. And I'd never give you my address, anyway.

Watcher55: It's a moot point in any case. You won't win. You're scared. You're scared to share your faith. You don't even know if you HAVE faith. You're scared of me.

JennSmiles: Don't flatter yourself.

Watcher55: I wouldn't think of it. Let us meet one week from tonight. Just think— it could be our final conversation.

JennSmiles: It will be. See you in a week, loser.

Strider77: Yeah, see you until it's time for you to step off for good.

Watcher55: We'll see....

Private Chat # 124

The Checkup

 PARTICIPANTS HERE: 3
Watcher55 • JennSmiles • Strider77

WATCHER55: Ah, my friends! Welcome! I've missed you both.

JENNSMILES: Whatever.

STRIDER77: Yeah, whatever. And hey, Watcher—I mean…loser, you better get used to missing us, because I know Jenn came through on her bet. Right, Jenn?

JENNSMILES: Uh…

WATCHER55: Yes, Jenn, let's see how our little experiment went. And remember, God is watching and listening. I'm sure you're tempted to lie, but I know that your Heavenly Father would want you to be honest.

JennSmiles: You make me sick, you know that?

Watcher55: Do I? Or is it your own sense of failure that ails you?

Strider77: Jenn? I'm confused here. You told me earlier in the week that you had a couple of good convos with that girl from your work. What's the name of that place again? Loosey-Juicy?

JennSmiles: The Juice Is Loose. And yeah, this girl Brenda and I started talking about life—love, relationships, the meaning of human existence—all that Chopra-Oprah stuff. But…

Watcher55: Yes?

JennSmiles: OK, will you stop gloating? You won this time, all right? But I want another shot at this. Maybe we can go double or nothing.

Watcher55: Perhaps. But first Lorri and I would like to hear how you failed.

JennSmiles: I didn't fail, OK? I just kinda ran out of time. You know, you have to wait for the right moment to share something so personal. Giving me only a week to find someone and start talking about life's most important topics? That wasn't fair.

WATCHER55: You accepted the deal. You didn't complain about its lack of fairness. In fact, YOU are the one who gloated—prematurely, I might add. You called me a loser. But it's you who lost. And as I said before, Strider and I are curious as to why.

STRIDER77: I guess I am curious, Jenn. What happened?

JENNSMILES: Well, Brenda and I started really sharing stuff, from our hearts, you know? Her home is a war zone, just like mine. We both agreed that we'd never get married if our parents' marriages are any indication of what it's like. But then…

WATCHER55: But then what, Jennifer?

JENNSMILES: I'm getting to it. Keep your shirt on! Well, I kinda mentioned, just in passing, that I go to church. I watched her face for some kind of reaction. And this look just came over her—like when you think you're biting into a piece of pure chocolate candy and instead it's filled with that coconut crap or that orange goo.

STRIDER77: That's pretty much my reaction whenever Blake raves about how cool church is. As far as I'm concerned, "church" and "cool" don't belong in the same sentence.

JENNSMILES: Well, you're definitely on the same page with Brenda. I asked her, "Is something wrong? Do you have something against church?" Then she says, "No, it's a free country and all; I just never took you for one of those." And, man, the way she said "those." It was like "those child molesters…those cannibals…those telemarketers."

WATCHER55: How did you respond? Did you deny your faith?

JENNSMILES: No, of course not! I just said, "I don't really know what you mean by 'those,' but I can tell it isn't good."

Then I said, "I'm just a person who experienced God's love for the first time, and it changed me. It rescued me." She just looked at me like I was speaking Latvian or something. So that's when I knew I had failed the challenge. So go ahead, Watcher. Bust my chops. Rub it in. But it doesn't change anything. God's love is still the most important thing in my world. And you're still a stalker freak.

WATCHER55: I'll forgive the insult because I know it springs from your sense of inadequacy. But I must call you on your claim that it doesn't change anything. It changes everything.

JENNSMILES: I don't see how.

WATCHER55: Listen to me, Jennifer: I am a teacher, a professor, in fact. And it's a proven axiom of education that you don't truly know a subject until you can teach it to others. Further, let's consider love. The very definition of love states that love is something that must be given. Love that is hoarded is not love at all.

JennSmiles: I don't disagree with anything you just said. But I'm not sure where you're going with it.

Watcher55: It's quite simple, really. If you weren't in such a religious haze, you would have already figured it out. Your so-called faith has clouded your ability to think clearly. Listen: If you truly knew what faith was all about, you would have been able to address Brenda's doubt and distaste. And if you truly loved her, you wouldn't have given up on her. You would have kept trying to save her soul. Don't you see what you did? You quit as soon as you knew your time limit was up and you were going to lose a bet. That's all that matters to you: winning a bet, not winning a lost soul to the Lord.

Strider77: I hate to say it, but I think he has a point, Jenn.

JennSmiles: Why are you both attacking me? What did I do to either one of you?

Watcher55: Don't get so defensive, Jennifer. We are both your friends. But friends tell each other the truth. And the truth in your case is simply this: You say that God's love is the most important thing in your life. In fact, you say that love saved your life. And you say it with conviction. I can feel the conviction in your words.

JENNSMILES: Well...I'm glad you do.

WATCHER55: But what happens when you try to share that godly love and faith with a co-worker and friend? It shatters. You see, it all SOUNDS good in your own head—or when you're at church with all the other brain-washed sheep. But when you try to share it in the real world, it kinda sounds hollow and contrived, doesn't it? And that heartfelt conviction just melts away under the harsh sun of reality.

JENNSMILES: No! That's not what happened. You're...you're twisting my words or something. Look—you have me all confused now! Can we just drop this whole thing? I need some time to think, to pray.

WATCHER55: Pray to whom, Jennifer? The invisible God behind your mirage of a faith? Where was God when you were witnessing to Brenda?

STRIDER77: You should listen to him, Jenn. He has a point. He's still a creep, but he has a point.

WATCHER55: I do indeed have a point. And, Jennifer, out of respect to you, I will drop this matter for now. But I urge you not to waste too much time mooning and praying over what has happened. It's time to move on—to get on with life in the real world. And that's where I can help.

JENNSMILES: I don't need your help. I don't need you around. I don't want you around.

WATCHER55: But you lost the bet. A bet that was in your power to win. So we're stuck with each other.

STRIDER77: Maybe not.

WATCHER55: What do you mean?

STRIDER77: How about a challenge for me? You might have gotten the best of Jenn, but I want a shot at the title. How about it, Watcher? Or are you scared?

WATCHER55: Please. Don't embarrass yourself, Lorri. You sound shrill and desperate.

STRIDER77: Yeah? Well, you sound like a chicken!

WATCHER55: I'll tell you what. Let's meet in exactly twenty-four hours. I want to give Jenn some time to contemplate her failure—or is it God's failure? Then, tomorrow night, Lorri, if you feel you are still up for a challenge, I have a delightful one planned just for you.

STRIDER77: I'll be here; you had better be too.

WATCHER55: Rest assured—I will be. And Jennifer, no hard feelings, OK?

JENNSMILES: No feelings at all, pinhead. See ya tomorrow.

Private Chat #125

The Strider Challenge

PARTICIPANTS HERE: 4
JennSmiles • Watcher55 • CrossKrys • Strider77

JENNSMILES: Krys, is it really you this time?

CROSSKRYS: Yep. Communicating from my own computer!

JENNSMILES: How did you get Bio Mom to spring for that? She hates 'puters, right?

CROSSKRYS: Right, but never underestimate the power of whining, my friend. Or of statements like, "But Dad lets me use his computer any time I want. And he's thinking of buying me a laptop." Drop a few bombs like that, and POOF! Biological Mom becomes Technological Mom.

WATCHER55: Excuse me for interrupting, but I believe an introduction is in order. Krys, we meet at last!

CROSSKRYS: Displeased to meet you.

WATCHER55: Such hostility from one of God's little lambs. I guess you haven't achieved that "peace that passes all understanding" level yet, eh?

CROSSKRYS: You are not going to bait me, Watcher. Jenn called me last night and told me all about you. First, I want you to know that I'm offended that you pretended to be me a while back. That was low. That was dishonest. You are a liar, plain and simple. And we're not going to lose sight of that fact. We're going to keep everything in perspective.

WATCHER55: I was merely playing a role, having some harmless fun. What—you've never pretended to be someone you're not? How much makeup are you wearing right now, Krys? How much work did you go to this morning to cover up the real you?

CrossKrys: You're good; I'll give you that. I want to jump all over what you just said, but that's what you want, isn't it? So I'm not going to give you the satisfaction. I am here for a purpose.

Watcher55: Let me guess: You're here to say, "Leave my widdo friends awone or I'm gonna tell on you!!!"

CrossKrys: No, I'm not here to threaten you. I am asking you, as a gentleman, to cease communication with my friends. No threat, just a request. And you are a gentleman, aren't you? I mean, you're not some pathetic hanger-on freak who is so starved for female attention that he has to harass teen girls, are you?

Watcher55: Who do you think that I am?

CrossKrys: I am still deciding that. It depends on your behavior. If you will show enough class and self-restraint to stop harassing my friends when you've been asked nicely, that's one thing. If not, then maybe you ARE just another loner-loser hiding behind a computer screen and preying on the innocent. Just an insecure, inept booty hound who can't get a girlfriend in real life, so he plays out sick fantasies on his computer. Why, Watcher? What's the matter—did your inflatable girlfriend spring a leak?

WATCHER55: My, oh my. Aren't you the little firecracker? I like your spunk, but you are so misguided. CrossKrys has her wires crossed. I am quite successful in life. I have all the women I want. You'd most likely be quite attracted to me, Krys. Assuming you have good taste, of course— or that you aren't planning to be a nun. That's a popular way for young Christians to repress their sexuality, is it not?

CROSSKRYS: You're going to dis nuns now? What's next? Puppies, baby harp seals, Jerry's kids? You're an adult, I take it?

WATCHER55: Yes.

CROSSKRYS: Interesting—you told Jenn and Lorri you were nineteen. Another lie. But I believe you're telling the truth now. You are a full-fledged adult. But given that fact, why aren't you throwing your challenges at fellow adults? Not man enough, perhaps?

WATCHER55: You better watch yourself, my friend. Don't play with fire.

JENNSMILES: Oooooh. Sounds like someone's losing his cool. What happened to the Rico Suave we used to know?

WATCHER55: Oh, I'm cool. Make no mistake. But I won't be disrespected. Not by some teenage Christian vermin.

STRIDER77: Hey, you're the one who disrespected my friend last night. And, Krys, what you're saying is cool and all, but last night I threw a challenge at this creep, and he backed down. I hate to interrupt— especially while Watcher is getting clowned—but I have a way to get rid of him for good.

WATCHER55: Or so you think.

STRIDER77: Bring it on, then, dude. Give me a challenge. Make me the same deal you made Jenn.

WATCHER55: You're too young, too weak, too naïve to take on a challenge from me. Jennifer had a fighting chance; although, as we all know, she failed. You, however, you're a punk. I'd annihilate you.

STRIDER77: You think? Step up, then, American Psycho! Break me off a challenge. I can deal with it. And I'll take the thousand bucks. I just need to think of a place to have you send it, because you aren't getting my home address. I wasn't born yesterday, you know.

CROSSKRYS: Stride, I don't know you nearly as well as Jenn does, but please trust me here. Don't play games with this guy. Let me deal with this, OK?

STRIDER77: I can't go for that, Krys. He can't punk me out like that. I can take any challenge he can throw down. So come on, Watcher. It's your move.

CROSSKRYS: Lorri! No! You need to listen to me. I got this one.

WATCHER55: Girls, girls, girls! Let's not have a catfight here. Let's not embarrass ourselves.

STRIDER77: Why don't you shut up—unless you have a challenge for me. I don't want to hear anything else from you.

WATCHER55: Deal.

CROSSKRYS: No! No deal!

WATCHER55: It could get me out of your lives forever.

CROSSKRYS: I don't care. No deal.

JENNSMILES: I don't know, K. I don't think this mook is going to leave us alone any other way. Let's at least hear him out first. If we don't like the sound of things, we don't have to agree.

STRIDER77: Yeah, Jenn's right. Besides, I can take this guy. Just don't ask me to pray or anything, Watcher. I'm not a Christian like these two. I don't believe in prayer. I don't believe in God either. So keep him outta my deal.

WATCHER55: Of course. I wouldn't send you on a task that you were ill-equipped to handle. No, Lorri, since you are so young, I'm going to make your challenge much easier than Jenn's.

STRIDER77: Hey! That's not fair! I'm tough beyond my age. I'm street-smart. Don't hold back—bring it on!

JENNSMILES: Lorri, hello? You're losing perspective here. The easier the challenge, the easier it will be to squash this guy.

STRIDER77: I just don't want something too easy. A challenge isn't a challenge if it's not hard.

WATCHER55: Hmmm. Well, on the surface, this one might not seem difficult, but…

CROSSKRYS: Lorri, for the last time: Don't play this guy's game. Let's all sign off right now. We don't HAVE to talk to this guy anymore, challenge or no challenge. We'll just block him from contacting us. That's all we have to do. Problem solved.

JennSmiles: That's true, I guess. Maybe we should just bounce outta here, Stride.

Watcher55: I guess you could try that if Lorri is truly that afraid of failure.

Strider77: Man, I'm sick of this! It's time to smack it up! I want to hear the challenge right now, Haddon, or maybe I will sign off and never talk to you again.

JennSmiles: LORRI!

Strider77: Just shut up, OK, Jenn? This is my life. My choice.

Watcher55: And all I want is one hour of your life. Tomorrow is Saturday. And if your repulsive little town is like most of those in America, there will be an assortment of parties tomorrow night, correct?

Strider77: Well, one of my friends from a couple blocks over, her sister is having a party. And there's this guy, Greg, there's almost always a party at his house. But I'm not allowed to go to parties.

WATCHER55: Well, then, I guess that this challenge is over before it began....

STRIDER77: Wait a minute—I said I wasn't allowed. That doesn't mean I won't go. I do plenty of things I'm not "allowed" to do. I sneak out all the time. And, you guys, if you tell Blake that, I'll personally kill both of you. The last thing I need is to give him another reason to harass me about "living a godly life." Puh-leeze. So, Watcher, I go to a party, right? Then what?

WATCHER55: That's it. You have a watch?

STRIDER77: I run distance. I have a chronograph. It's waterproof too in case you care.

WATCHER55: Good for you. All you need to do is get to the party and check your precious little chronograph. Then, one hour later, you may leave.

STRIDER77: That's it? Come on, dude, what's the catch? I don't have to drink? I don't have to make out with a stranger?

WATCHER55: Don't get cocky, my little runner friend. An hour is a long time. A lot can happen.

JENNSMILES: For the first time tonight, he's right. A LOT can happen. I can tell you from experience.

CROSSKRYS: Listen to the voice of experience, Lorri. Besides, why defy your parents? I am sure that they love you, and it would break their hearts if they knew you disobeyed them like this!

STRIDER77: OK, so, like, did Blake brainwash both of you? You sound so much like him that it's trippin' me out. Besides, I'm sure a little nighttime covert op won't break their hearts. And even if it did, they're just like Blake. They have Jesus to fix their broken hearts.

JENNSMILES: Lorri, you shouldn't make light of that. You have no idea what it's like to get your broken heart mended.

STRIDER77: You're right. I don't. Because my heart is strong. It doesn't need fixing. And my will is strong too.

Watcher, I'm sneaking out and going to a party tomorrow. It's not like I haven't done it before. I'll hang for an hour, no problem. You can make it two if you want. So the day after tomorrow at, let's say 11:00 A.M., when my parents are at church and I'm NOT, we can settle up.

WATCHER55: Agreed. But there is one more thing....

STRIDER77: <heavy sigh> What is it?

WATCHER55: Well, when Jenn lost, I didn't ask for anything in victory—save for the privilege of conversing with you young ladies for at least a bit longer. But since we're on to challenge number two, the stakes must go up a bit.

CROSSKRYS: I knew this was coming. Let's log off—NOW! Please, Lorri and Jenn.

JENNSMILES: I guess you're right, Krys. I am starting to get a weird vibe off this guy. When I count three, we're out, OK?

STRIDER77: Whatever. I'm getting hungry, so OK.

JENNSMILES: One...

WATCHER55: Please don't go.

JENNSMILES: Two...three!

JENNSMILES: I can't believe Krys fell for that.

STRIDER77: I can. She's gullible. Just like Blake. So if I lose—which I won't— what do you want in return, Watcher?

WATCHER55: Please, call me Haddon. You were using my name for a while, but then you stopped.

STRIDER77: Whatever. Haddon. Anyway, what do you want?

WATCHER55: Just a picture of you.

STRIDER77: Let me guess—in my undies, right? Or do you prefer nude? I'll check the family albums and see what I can find. I think I might have posed nude for our family Christmas card last year....

WATCHER55: Please, Lorri! What do you take me for? I'm not like that at all. A simple headshot will be fine. One of your school pictures.

JENNSMILES: OK, I don't like this. I don't like the thought of this guy knowing what you look like. Maybe we should think this over, Stride.

STRIDER77: No need, Jenn. I'm all over this. It's a deal, Haddon.

JENNSMILES: Lorri, are you sure you know what you're doing?

STRIDER77: Relax. He isn't getting any picture, because he isn't going to win. See ya in about thirty-six hours, loser. And I promise not to rub it in too much when I smoke ya.

WATCHER55: That's very sporting of you.

JENNSMILES: Just so you understand what's at stake here, Haddon. You lose, you're gone.

WATCHER55: That is the deal. If I lose, I'll abide by it. Good evening, ladies. And good luck, Lorri. You will need it. Lots of it. Lots of luck and prayers.

STRIDER77: I don't believe in prayer.

WATCHER55: Then I guess you're on your own.

JENNSMILES: She might not pray, but I will.

WATCHER55: Oh my, I'm so afraid now. Lorri! Lorri! Won't you please recuse yourself from this agreement? Jennifer here is going to PRAY! She's going to talk to an invisible man who she thinks lives somewhere up in the sky! What chance do I have against such a preposterous superstition?

JENNSMILES: I guess we'll see soon. Lorri, like it or not, I'm prayin' for ya.

STRIDER77: Save your prayers, baby. I got this down cold. See ya both in thirty-six.

Private Chat #126

The Ace Case

PARTICIPANTS HERE: 2
Watcher55 • A.C.008

A.C.008: Hey, where is everyone? Jenn said she and her crew would be here.

WATCHER55: Sorry, waste product. I fixed it so that they can't get in. It's just you and I.

A.C.008: Well, who are you, foo?

WATCHER55: Don't call me a fool, you piece of human garbage! Which one of us has a mind and body polluted by drugs? Who spends every day on an all-consuming conquest to get high?

A.C.008: Neither one of us right now. I'm tryin' to get level. I don't roll like that anymore.

WATCHER55: Ace, please. You, level? How many days since you last got high—or should I say, how many hours?

A.C.008: Two days. That's a start.

WATCHER55: Ha! C'mon, dawg, if I may call you "dawg." How long before you slide back into the comfortable cesspool that is your life, your destiny?

A.C.008: I don't think that way. I'm not predicting the future. My plan is to get through today. That's all I can do.

WATCHER55: You're wasting your time and effort—and what few brain cells you have remaining. Let me speak in a way you can understand: *How you feel, Jack?* Be honest, Ace, isn't every cell in your body crying out for some of the sticky-icky-icky? Or is rock your drug of choice? Do you rock the rock? Or maybe you're an X-man—is that it, Ace? Are you a raver?

A.C.008: It's not your business. What's your game, foo?

WATCHER55: I don't play games. I'm here to warn you. Stay away—from Blake, Jenn, and the whole Scooby gang. I don't want you around. They don't want you around either. You disgust all of us.

A.C.008: Whatever. I don't care what you think. And them? I think you're lying. They don't roll like that. They don't hate on me. Drugs or no drugs.

WATCHER55: Sure—just keep telling yourself that. Meanwhile, you had better start caring what I think, you worthless burnout! Just go back to getting high and stay out of our world. The real world's no place for you. Come on, you know you're going to slide eventually. Why torture yourself in the meantime? I know thousands of people just like you; no one makes it out. No one. That's a myth perpetrated by those "Macramé—my anti-drug" idiots. Ace, just imagine it: Think about that warm, safe, peaceful place you can go to. The place where you rule. The place where all troubles melt away. You could go there right now. No one will care if you do.

A.C.008: Why don't you step off?

WATCHER55: What's wrong, Ace? The truth getting to you?

A.C.008: I am trying to change. And in my program, they tell me to avoid people like you.

WATCHER55: That's one thing I agree with "them" about. Avoid me. And I am spending a lot of time with your cyber friends, so if you avoid them, you'll avoid me.

A.C.008: And if I don't?

WATCHER55: I will make your life hell. You have no idea. I know I've already made you uneasy, tense. I bet you're so keyed up now that you'll HAVE to get high before the day's end. You haven't got a prayer.

A.C.008: I'm not listening to you.

WATCHER55: Sure you are. You know I'm right. You're jonesin' so bad right now, aren't you? Don't lie.

A.C.008: Just go away.

WATCHER55: I will if you will. You've had just a taste of my power. If you don't want to be tearing your own flesh from your body, back off. If you try to join even one of our chats, I'll fry you. If you send one email to Jenn, Blake, any of them, I'll know. I'm watching you. And you will pay. There is no drug that will bring you relief from the hell I'll unleash on you. Now, run along, Martin. That's your real name, remember? MARTIN! No wonder you go by Ace. Now, disappear. You don't matter anyway. No one will miss you. Consider it, Ace: Relief is close at hand. You know where to find it. Don't fight the inevitable.

A.C.008: Shut up, OK? I'm out. You're freakin' me.

WATCHER55: Good. You're gone. Good-bye, my pathetic little waste product. I know what you're going to do right now. I hope you OD and die.

Private Chat #127

Strider's Reckoning

Participants Here: 5
Watcher55 • JennSmiles • Strider77 • Blake7 • CrossKrys

WATCHER55: Ah, Blake, the super-Christian. I'm honored to meet you at last. And what a perfect time for your first encounter with me. I promise you it will be memorable.

BLAKE7: Who are you? Are you man enough to step out from behind your screen name and tell me who you are?

STRIDER77: Never mind that! Hey—who invited HIM here? Log off, Blake. Get on your bike and ride. Pedal on to the next state on your Big Bike Tour. And don't forget to keep the post-cards comin'. Mom and Dad lap 'em up. I get to have 'em read out loud to me at dinnertime, right after the mandatory five-minute prayer. I guess I'll be in college before I get to eat a hot meal.

Blake7: Lorri, please…

Strider77: Oh, give me a break! You're going to whine now? Plead? I don't want to hear it, OK? Just step off. This has nothing to do with you. This is all about my life, my choices.

Blake7: Lorri, you're my little sister. I care about you. So does Krys. So does Jenn. That's why she called me on my cell and told me I HAD to be here today.

Strider77: Thanks a lot, Jenn! I hate you!

JennSmiles: I don't hate you, Lorri. Quite the opposite, in fact. That's why I reached out to your bro. We need him in this room. We need the big guns to deal with Haddon.

Strider77: Blake? A big gun? Ha! He's got no guns. He's got no game. That's why you fold like a beach chair in the big races, isn't it, my brother? You're nothing but a lot of talk and a bible.

BLAKE7: That's Bible, with a capital B, Lorri. You need to show God's Word the proper respect.

STRIDER77: I'll spell it any way I want to. You can't stop me, and neither can God—I mean god.

WATCHER55: Welcome to Family Feud! Go on, Lorri, keep telling your brother how you really feel about him and his sham of a religion.

STRIDER77: Why don't you put a sock in it, Haddon? I don't know why you're so freakin' giddy. I hate you almost as much as I hate Blake!

WATCHER55: Why hate me? I'm not the one who force-fed you religion all your life. I'm not the one who acted superior to you all the time, who looked at you with that sour mixture of pity and contempt in his eyes.

STRIDER77: No, but you're the one who got me to go to that party, and I'll never forgive you for that.

WATCHER55: You think I want your forgiveness? You think I even care about your forgiveness? You are more naïve than I thought. However, I am curious to know what happened at the party. My, oh my. I hope nothing went awry. I hope you didn't put yourself in harm's way. Why, I'd never forgive myself. Oh—wait, that's right, I don't care about forgiveness. I don't care what happened to you. But I think your fellow vermin here do. So spill the beans, punk!

STRIDER77: I hate you!

WATCHER55: I hate you right back, you little she-pig. But hey, you were talking tough thirty-six hours ago. What about now? How tough do you feel now?

JENNSMILES: Oh, Lorri, what happened? Are you OK?

BLAKE7: Lorri, please tell me you're all right!

STRIDER77: No, I'm not OK, OK? You knew, didn't you, Haddon? Somehow you were in on this. You're the one who's a pig!

JennSmiles: Lorri—what's going on? What happened? Tell us about it; we can help you.

Strider77: No, you can't. No one can. I thought I had an easy grand—and Haddon out of our lives forever. I snuck out of the house, no problem, just like always. My parents go to bed at like nine every night so they can get up early and start "serving the Lord." Anyway, I met my friend Bri outside and we went to Greg's party.

Blake7: Lorri, you went to a party at Greg's house? That guy is insane!

Strider77: I was talkin' here, Blake. Or don't you want to hear the gory details?

Watcher55: Please, Lorri, continue.

Strider77: So the party was like no big deal, really. Just lots of noise, lots of beer, and a few people burning blunts. This guy, Tom, he pours beers for Bri and me. Then, after a while, he asks us if we'd like to get away from all the noise. We were like, "sure," because this hip-hop music was bangin' so loud that it was giving us a headache. And we were starting to feel kinda woozy or something.

JennSmiles: Where did you go, Lorri? Please tell me it wasn't to a bedroom!

Strider77: OK, I won't tell you that. I won't tell you that I must have passed out in that room that I won't tell you about. I won't tell you that when I woke up on this bed, Tom was standing there, laughing. I found Bri—she was passed out on the floor. I grabbed her and we staggered out of there. Tom was following behind us, still laughing. He kept saying, "Thanks for everything, girls! Thanks for EVERYTHING!"

Watcher55: Tom sounds like such a grateful young man. One doesn't often find manners like that amongst today's youth.

Blake7: Watcher, you are a dead man. I'm talking to a dead man!

Watcher55: Those are strange words, coming from one who claims to serve the

Prince of Peace. You're supposed to turn the other cheek. Or in this case, give me another sister. Too bad for me that you don't have one.

BLAKE7: I'll deal with you later, Watcher. Lorri, please log off right now, and I'll call you from my cell.

STRIDER77: I don't want to talk to you, Blake. I don't want to talk to anyone.

BLAKE7: You know I'm going to have to call Mom and Dad about this.

STRIDER77: Well, they're not here right now. They're at church, and then they'll be off volunteering on one of their five dozen church committees. So go ahead and leave a message, but I'll just erase it. That's what I did with the last few you left.

BLAKE7: Lorri, they are your parents. They need to know. I'll call Dad at work if that's what I have to do.

STRIDER77: Go ahead. I'll just deny anything happened.

WATCHER55: Ah, but that wouldn't be the case, would it, Lorri? Hey, I'm curious: What time was it when you and your little vermin friend left the party?

STRIDER77: Well, I am glad you brought that up. It was more than an hour after we arrived, which means I win the bet. So at least I'm rid of you.

WATCHER55: Perhaps you did win. And what makes me saddest about that is that I won't get a picture of you. I would have loved to have one. I would have kept it close to me always. That way, I could look at it and remind myself of what you looked like BEFORE you lost your innocence.

JENNSMILES: You are a devious, conniving, lying snake! You are pure evil!

WATCHER55: You flatter me.

JENNSMILES: You disgust me.

WATCHER55: I do? Well, no worries. You'll learn to appreciate me in time. I tend to grow on people.

JENNSMILES: Wait a minute: There is no "in time." Stride won the bet. You're out. A deal is a deal.

WATCHER55: Perhaps. But you see, I was operating upon the understanding that our Miss Lorri would be an active participant in the party. She fell asleep on the job, as it were. You know, as I think about it, I must rescind my concession from earlier. I'm going to pull an Al Gore. Technically, I don't think Lorri met the challenge. But just to show I'm a good sport, I won't make her send me a picture. But you're not getting rid of me. We've become so close. Of course, not as close as "Tom" and who knows how many of his friends have become to your baby sister, Blake....

BLAKE7: You...

WATCHER55: There's no need to thank me for my magnanimity, Blake. That's just the kind of guy I am.

STRIDER77: ENOUGH! I'm sick of every single one of you. I'm out. And I might not come back. Good night.

August 13

Secret Session #2

 PARTICIPANTS HERE: 2
Watcher55 • Ghost9

WATCHER55: I don't remember when I've been happier.

GHOST9: Please don't get all giddy on me. You're annoying when you're giddy, remember?

WATCHER55: Well, I can't help but be pleased with last night. That Strider77 delivered a spectacular perform-ance. I thought our old buddy Blake was going to die of a broken heart right there on the spot.

GHOST9: A quick death like that would have been too good for him. Remember, we need to make him SUFFER.

WATCHER55: Oh, he's going to suffer, don't worry. The heartache he's feeling now is only the beginning. We're going to compound that, multiply it, and throw a few more evil numbers into the equation. His nightmare has only begun.

GHOST9: Good.

WATCHER55: Good, indeed. Blake will soon curse the day he was born. Maybe he'll curse God too.

GHOST9: I'd love to be able to hear that.

WATCHER55: You will. All in due time. See you in ten days.

Private Chat # 128

The Trouble With Lorri

 PARTICIPANTS HERE: 3
JennSmiles • CrossKrys • Blake7

BLAKE7: Thanks for meeting me here, my friends. I am just so torn up. I don't know what to do.

CROSSKRYS: We're here for you, B.

JENNSMILES: Yeah, just let us know what you need.

BLAKE7: I wish I knew. I managed to get Lorri on the phone earlier today. She hates me, I'm afraid, but she's also hurting.

JENNSMILES: B, I don't mean to pry, but do you think, at the party, that she was…you know?

BLAKE7: She says she can't be sure. I told her this needs to be reported to the police. She needs to get medical attention. But she says no way. She keeps saying she will deny everything if I tell anybody. I don't know whether to call my dad or what. She says she will never speak to me again if I do. I feel like I'm trapped in a room, and the walls are pushing in on me. This thing, I fear it's going to crush me.

CROSSKRYS: I think you need to head home.

BLAKE7: I'm way ahead of you. I'm taking a bus back later today. I'll be home in a few days.

JENNSMILES: Why not fly, B?

BLAKE7: Believe me, I wish I could. But I spent almost all my money on this bike trip. And I hate to ask my parents. I know they are in credit card debt up to their eyeballs. Sure, Dad would spring for a ticket in an emergency, but then I'd have to tell him the details. And then Lorri would never speak to me. I'd lose my sister. I've thought about calling someone at the church too. But there's no way someone would give me that kind of money without telling my parents.

JENNSMILES: But you'll have to tell your parents something, no matter how you get home.

BLAKE7: I know. But I can just tell them that I got homesick. Or that I'm injured. Neither of those would be a lie. I'm injured more than I've ever been.

CROSSKRYS: I don't want to give you false hope, B. But maybe it was just a cruel prank this guy pulled on Lorri. Maybe he just played a mind game on her. After all, she's only thirteen. I mean, what kind of lowlife would do something so awful to someone who's barely a teenager?

BLAKE7: You don't know Greg. If this Tom guy is anything like him, there's no conscience involved.

JENNSMILES: What are you going to do when you get home?

BLAKE7: Find Tom.

CrossKrys: And then…

Blake7: You know, I better not say. That would be putting you guys, and myself, in a bad position.

CrossKrys: Blake, I don't like the sound of this. Look, if you go after this guy, that isn't going to solve anything. Believe me, I have no sympathy for him, and I hope that he gets such a bad case of VD someday that his skin rots off. But you, you can't get all ghetto about this.

JennSmiles: She's right, B. You can't roll with the violence, man. Your sister needs you, whether she admits it or not. And you can't help her if you're in jail or in the hospital.

CrossKrys: Or in the morgue.

Blake7: So you think this guy would smoke me? Thanks a lot, Krys!

JennSmiles: Hey, B, give Krys a break. No one's insulting your manhood here. We're just saying that anybody who would abuse a junior-high girl probably wouldn't have a problem shankin'—or gattin'—her big brother. Besides, B, doesn't the Bible talk about vengeance belonging to God?

BLAKE7: <sigh> Yes, it does, Jenn.

JENNSMILES: Well, I know I'm just a neophyte Christian here, but if that's what the Book says, maybe we should leave the revenge stuff in God's hands.

CROSSKRYS: Jenn is right. God doesn't need our help with vengeance. But it seems that He does enlist our help when it comes to comfort, love, and support. And that's what your sis needs—even more than seeing that Tom dude strung up by his boy parts.

BLAKE7: I guess you're right. Man, how did you two get so mature?

JENNSMILES: We had a good teacher. And a good friend.

CROSSKRYS: Ditto that.

BLAKE7: Thanks. Both of you. I gotta go now. There's a Greyhound with my name on it. The next time we chat, I'll be on Cali time.

JENNSMILES: Peace to you, my friend. And you know the kind of peace I'm talking about, because you're the one who taught me about it: Peace isn't the absence of pain but the presence of God.

CROSSKRYS: Amen. And, B, you have our digits, so call us from your cell if you need to talk, rant, cry, or whatever.

BLAKE7: You are true friends. Thank you. We'll talk soon.

Private Chat #129

Sifting Through the Rubble

PARTICIPANTS HERE: 3
CrossKrys • Blake7 • JennSmiles

JENNSMILES: B, you back home?

BLAKE7: Yeah, if you can call it a home right now.

CROSSKRYS: How is Lorri? How are your parents? How is…everything? Who knows what?

BLAKE7: Lorri is pretty good, considering. She is begging me not to talk to our parents about anything. So far, I'm respecting her wishes. But I'm begging her to get some kind of help—physical, emotional, mental. I wish I could add spiritual to that list, but I know that's out of the question for right now. She said this morning, "If God loves me, like you say, then why did He let this happen to me?" And she says what's worse is that she doesn't even know what "this" is.

JennSmiles: I am so worried about her. And you're right—you've got to get her to a doctor, at the very least.

Blake7: I know. I know. Meanwhile, I am tracking down Tom.

CrossKrys: B, don't forget what we said about vengeance!

Blake7: I haven't forgotten. I promise. But I need to get him to tell me the extent of what happened. I must know exactly what we're dealing with. I need to know what Lorri is at risk for.

CrossKrys: Do you think he'll talk?

Blake7: I don't know. I will appeal to his sense of decency, assuming he has any. If that doesn't work, I'm sorry, guys, but I might have to start breaking bones.

CROSSKRYS: Come on, Blake. You're better than that.

JENNSMILES: She's right, B. Nothing good can come from you bringing the war on that guy.

BLAKE7: But you two don't understand! You don't know how it feels!

WATCHER55: Hi, everyone. I hope I'm not interrupting anything important. Hmmm, I'm just scrolling up the screen.... It seems that there's some tension here. It seems that the soul mates are at odds.

JENNSMILES: Who cares what it seems like to you, freak?

WATCHER55: I'm a freak? It's your friend Blake who is freakish. And pathetic. His world is crumbling around him. Everything he claimed to believe in has collapsed.

BLAKE7: That's not true.

WATCHER55: Sure it is. Thank hell for guys like you, Blake. You talk a good game, but you ultimately become the best advertisements for the hollowness of Christianity. When you're faced with a true challenge from life, you run out of answers, don't you?

Blake7: I'm not out of answers.

Watcher55: Really? Then how about a little debate? Your Christianity against my real-world, street-tested truth.

JennSmiles: This isn't fair. Blake is hurting. This is no time to work your twisted mojo on him.

Watcher55: I thought Christians were supposed to be good in a crisis. Doesn't God promise to be strong, even when you are weak?

Blake7: You know what? Bring it on! You have something to say to me? You have some hard questions to ask? Let's hear them!

Watcher55: Fine. Under one condition. Your sister sits in with you.

BLAKE7: Deal. But I have a condition of my own: You start attacking her, trying to humiliate her, and the conversation's over. So get ready to hit me with your best shot. I'll go get Lorri. Let's reconvene in about fifteen.

Private Chat #130

Blake Battles Watcher

PARTICIPANTS HERE: 5
JennSmiles • CrossKrys • Strider77 • Blake7 • Watcher55

WATCHER55: Are you ready, Blake? Are you ready to have your sham faith exposed in front of people you care deeply about?

BLAKE7: My faith is real. You're not going to expose anything but your own weaknesses. You're wrong about my faith.

WATCHER55: I'm wrong? Then how come most of the world agrees with me? Let's take my first case in point. Watch your TV for any amount of time. Do you see any advertisements for products that make one a more moral person? Do the richest and most powerful companies in the world manufacture virtue? No, of course not. There's no market for it.

JennSmiles: I don't see what you're getting at—you can't sell virtue, because you can't buy it.

Watcher55: Believe me, if there was a market for it, someone would figure out how to make it and sell it. But that's not what people want. They want sleek, fast cars. They want clothes that show their good taste and their surgically and health-club-enhanced physiques. They want light beer so that their heads can get light without their bodies getting heavy. They want SMART FINANCIAL ADVICE so that they can make more and more money. People want success. And success is about getting what you want. Feeling good. Looking good. Eating well. Living well. And sex. Lots and lots of sex. On video and DVD. On in-demand TV—in the comfort of your motel room, in the privacy of your home.

Blake7: But you're wrong about success, Watcher. And so are all the people that peddle all the crap you're talking about. Material wealth is an oxymoron as far as I am concerned. It's just a bunch of stuff. It's metal, plastic, silicone, empty thrills, and fermented liquids. What does it really do for the quality of your life? And what are you going to do with all that stuff when you die? What good will it do you in the long run?

WATCHER55: But, my dear Blake, what if there is no "long run"? What if you deprive yourself of material pleasures your whole life, only to find out there is no hereafter? What a waste! Get it now; it's your only chance. Get tanned, get rich, get drunk, get high, and, yes, get laid! Do what you need to do to feel good. It's insane to follow a bunch of rules that serve only to deprive you of feeling good.

BLAKE7: Following God's standards will only improve the quality of your life. Look how many self-indulgent people are also self-destructive. How come so many "successful" entertainers and athletes keep committing crimes, abusing drugs, failing at love, catching diseases? Come on, Watcher, the Depressed, Alcoholic, Out-of-Control Millionaire is practically a cliché. I wish Kurt Cobain, Tupac, Jim Morrison, Marilyn Monroe, Jimi Hendrix, Chris Farley, Freddie Mercury, John Belushi, and a host of others were here to refute your philosophy. But they can't make it this evening. They're all dead because they lived life your way. What you call God's depriving, I call His protection.

WATCHER55: I knew you'd bring "him" into this sooner or later. But please! How weak-minded to think you need some big "daddy" to protect you from your own fun! Life is to be enjoyed. We are free, sovereign beings. Maybe some of those people you named died a bit young. But I bet they went with smiles on their faces. You think they'd be happier if they were sitting in some Christian nursing home today, singing "Kum Ba Yah" and ingesting their dinners through one tube and excreting them through another? No! Far better that they lived free and died free!

BLAKE7: Free? Can you smell the big stinky pile of lies you're creating? Freedom does not equal chaos! True freedom isn't just to follow whatever reckless notion one has at a given time. True freedom comes from the power to make your own choices and making the wise ones—the godly ones. Freedom always comes with responsibility. By definition, true freedom requires self-control. If you're always out of control, that's not freedom. That's being a slave to chaos and disorder. It's like running down a mountain, out of control. It might be a thrill for a while. But eventually you're gonna crash. You think those people I mentioned were free? Get real! They were prisoners of a lifestyle—or should I say deathstyle?

JENNSMILES: And I want to add to the truth Blake is throwing down. Listen to me, Watcher. I wasn't free before I met God. I was a prisoner too. I was a prisoner of other people's perception of me. I was a prisoner to my low self-esteem and all I did trying to make other people like me. I was like a circus animal: well-trained in the ways of pleasing others, but deeply, deeply unhappy.

WATCHER55: And now you'll jump through all kinds of hoops to make God like you. You're still a prisoner. You have merely exchanged jailers.

JENNSMILES: Wrong answer, Botcher—I mean, Watcher. I didn't have to do anything to make God love me. He just does. It just took a while—and a bit of divine intervention—to help me realize that love was out there, searching for me. Once I realized it, I did just like my boyz in dc Talk say it: I took a love-plunge into God's arms. And I'm never leaving. Not for all the money, power, fame, or prestige in the world.

CROSSKRYS: Rock on, Jenn! Are you gettin' this, Watcher? Are you taking notes? Because there will be a test! Are you gonna be ready for it?

WATCHER55: Let's switch gears a bit, OK? I'm not conceding anything; I just want to pursue some different angles here.

JENNSMILES: What you want is for Blake to go to a neutral corner, because he's pummeling your sorry butt.

BLAKE7: No, Jenn, it's OK. We'll extend you some grace, Watcher. Go ahead.

WATCHER55: Very well, then. You Christians often refer to God as your "Father." Well, why wouldn't this "Father" want all his kids to have whatever they want? Why would he want them to be deprived of all the good things in life? Jenn, to your point, why not have God AND all the best that the world has to offer? Why do you have to give up what's good when you accept God?

JENNSMILES: Let him have it again, Blake. He's still not getting it.

BLAKE7: I'm all over it, Jenn. Watcher, how tragic that you think "the good things" are man-made, with designer labels and high price tags. And as for letting kids have whatever they want…do you know parents who actually let their kids have everything they want? Eat what they want, do whatever they please, buy whatever they want, via Mom and Dad's credit cards? I do. And guess what that kind of parenting produces: The most miserable, bratty kids in the world. Kids who grow up to become unhappy, self-centered, destructive adults.

WATCHER55: Come on, Blake—you have to admit that possessions make us happy. They make us feel good. Gordon Gecko said it well in the movie *Wall Street: "Greed is good."* It always feels good to get more, whether it's money, cars, fame, or sex.

BLAKE7: There's a word for Gecko's philosophy. It's called selfishness. The happiest people I know are, by far, the least selfish people I know. Be real, Watcher. How many happy selfish people do YOU know? Really happy people who feel good about who they are and aren't constantly hustling to fill some yawning void in their lives? The Bible says it well: He who loves money will never have enough. I've seen it over and over. Greedy people think they own their possessions, but in truth, it's the other way around.

WATCHER55: I will grant you that some people can't handle success, can't truly enjoy the fun that their possessions bring. But those people just aren't self-actualized, as I am. They simply aren't evolved.

BLAKE7: Really? You're happy, Watcher?

WATCHER55: Of course. I am a happy, centered individual who enjoys all the finer things in life—without a shred of guilt, I might add.

BLAKE7: I don't think you're being honest with us, or yourself. Come on, Watcher, what's your void? Why are you harassing my sister and her friends? You're hurting them, scaring them, even putting them in danger. These are people who have done you no harm. And yet you torment them. Does that really make you happy? Does it fulfill you? Or are you driven to hurt others because you've been hurt your-self? Or maybe you're trying to please someone. Maybe some-one's pulling your strings. But whatever the case, you are selfish.

WATCHER55: I wouldn't call myself selfish.

BLAKE7: Yeah, that makes sense. Selfish people have a hard time admitting their faults.

WATCHER55: Stop using that word—it's a term one would apply to a baby, not a self-actualized adult like me.

JENNSMILES: Hey, dude, if the label fits…

WATCHER55: Silence, witch! Listen to me, all of you: I will not be analyzed by a pack of teenage Christian cretins! My motivations are none of your business.

BLAKE7: So you don't like people meddling in your business?

WATCHER55: Of course not, idiot.

Blake7: Well, now you know how we feel. You've invaded our lives. You've asked probing questions, and you've thrown down dangerous, personal challenges. But you're not man enough to face a few questions of your own?

Watcher55: How dare you question my manhood, my power, boy! I am MORE than a man. If only you knew whom you are messing with. You'd be trembling right now.

Blake7: If that is so, tell us who you are and watch me quake. That should be fun for you if you're really the kind of person you say you are. Come on, give us some answers: Who are you? Are you really happy and fulfilled? Are you proud of what your life stands for?

Watcher55: I don't see the relevance of your questions.

Blake7: I am asking about the purpose of your existence and your feelings about it—you don't find that relevant?

WATCHER55: Well, then…Give me a moment to gather my thoughts, and I shall answer you.

JENNSMILES: Whoa! Fresh outta snappy comebacks, Botcher? Dude, you are so gettin' played!

BLAKE7: Jenn, please, let's give him a moment to think. I think that's fair. These are big questions. I know I would want to think carefully before I answered. Haddon, if that's your real name, we'll wait for your answer. I'm sorry if I was rushing you.

WATCHER55: I don't have to answer you. You mean nothing to me. You aren't worthy of my answers.

BLAKE7: Fair enough. But know this: It's not important whether or not I matter to you, but we will all have to answer to God. And He asks some of the same questions I posed to you. You will have to answer not just with words but with your life and how you spend it. You're obviously intelligent and persuasive. You know a lot about computers; that's evident as well. But what are you doing with your gifts? You're hurting innocent people. Is this really what you want to do with your life? Is this really what you're all about?

WATCHER55: How I live my life is none of your affair, Christian pig!

BLAKE7: When it affects my sister, who is sitting here beside me now, your life does become my affair. Listen to me: Leave her alone. Leave us alone. You could be doing something good with your gifts. You could make people's lives better, instead of worse. And that would give you lasting joy, peace of mind. You wouldn't be so angry and hateful anymore. Please, think about what I've said. I will pray for you.

WATCHER55: Don't you dare! I don't want your prayers!

BLAKE7: But you need them.

WATCHER55: This was supposed to be a battle of wits and a battle of wills. But you're trying to turn it into a prayer meeting. I won't be lured into your trap. Good night!

JennSmiles: Wow, good job, B! You schooled that freak!

Strider77: Save your congrats, Jenn. Blake just got up and left the room. And he didn't look like he'd just won something. He looked distressed and really, really tired. It was weird; I thought he'd be all stoked after abusing Watcher.

CrossKrys: Maybe you don't know him as well as you thought you did….

Strider77: Maybe. Anyway, I'm kinda worried. I think I'll go check on him. I'm out.

Secret Session #3

 PARTICIPANTS HERE: 2
Watcher55 • Ghost9

GHOST9: Hello again, Watcher—or should I call you "Cigarette"? 'Cuz you sure got smoked the other night. I can smell the stank all the way from here.

WATCHER55: It wouldn't be wise of you to anger me right now.

GHOST9: I'm the one who should be angry. We had a deal. You're supposed to humiliate Blake in front of his friends. You were supposed to torture him till he raged against God, perhaps even denied God. Instead, he is praying for you. He's trying to counsel you. You're supposed to be this great teacher. He made you a student.

WATCHER55: Well, Ghost, I'm not done yet. Besides, Blake has suffered. I've been monitoring his emails and

IMs to his friends, to his youth pastor. His heart is ripped asunder by what happened to poor little Lorri. Come on, Ghost, you're closer to ground zero than I am—surely you can see the pain in his eyes, can't you?

GHOST9: Sure, I see the signs. And you're right; he's hurting, big-time. But pain is only part of your mission. I want more. I still want more. I want him busted up good, understand? I want him to turn his back on this whole God thing. I want to see him shaking his fists at the sky, spitting at the heavens.

WATCHER55: ☺

GHOST9: Why the cheesy smile?

WATCHER55: Just wait till you see what I'm gonna do next! It's gonna be a bloodbath.

GHOST9: I hope so. But that's what you said would happen with Tom. You said Blake would go after Tom and one of them would end up in the hospital or jail. That didn't happen. You know this if you've been monitoring his communication as closely as I have. You know what he's saying: "Bringing the war on Tom isn't going to help my sister. It will only make things worse." I can't stand it when he talks like that! It's infuriating! It's not human!

WATCHER55: Calm down, Ghost. As I said: Be patient and wait for the bloodbath.

GHOST9: Bloodbath, huh? I like the sound of that. But be careful—I want his pain to be more emotional and spiritual than physical. If I just wanted him beaten up, I could find any brain-dead hood to do that. You're supposed to operate at a higher level, remember? Besides, bruises heal.

WATCHER55: What's wrong, Ghost? Getting a bit squeamish, are you? Losing your edge?

GHOST9: I'm not losing anything. I'm just saying stick to the rules we agreed on.

WATCHER55: Don't talk to me about rules. I'm above rules. I'm above law. I'll do whatever I please. Let's not forget who has the real power here.

GHOST9: Right back atcha, Watcher. It's reality-check time: You don't do this my way, you don't get what I promised.

WATCHER55: You are so naïve, Ghost. What makes you think I need anything from you anymore? How do you know that I don't already have what I need?

GHOST9: You're bluffing. I know what you want.

WATCHER55: Do you? I guess we'll see. Sweet dreams, Ghost.

GHOST9: Watcher, don't go yet! We're not done here. What do you mean by what you just said? Watcher? Watcher?!

Private Chat #131

The Rematch

 PARTICIPANTS HERE: 2
Blake7 • Watcher55

BLAKE7: I'm glad you agreed to meet me here. And I promise—it'll be just the two of us, as you requested.

WATCHER55: Good.

BLAKE7: So have you thought about our conversation last week?

WATCHER55: Not really. I have better things to think about.

BLAKE7: Are you being honest?

WATCHER55: Why would I want to waste my time contemplating outdated Christian fairy-tale rubbish? "I'll pray for you"—what a pathetic sentiment!

BLAKE7: I did pray.

Watcher55: It didn't work.

Blake7: How can you say that? You don't know what I prayed for.

Watcher55: Enough! I didn't come here to rehash a week-old conversation. I have a more pressing matter to discuss with you.

Blake7: What could be more important than contemplating your destiny?

Watcher55: Contemplating YOUR destiny— which isn't looking too hopeful, as you're about to discover.

Blake7: I'm listening.

Watcher55: Good. I'll give you one thing, my friend; you're a formidable enemy. Those I answer to have been concerned about you for the past few years. You are becoming dangerous.

Blake7: You mentioned "those" you answer to. Remember, you ultimately answer to God. No one else.

WATCHER55: Silence! Don't keep bringing him up. I'm warning you; you don't want to anger me. Now, I have a bargain to discuss with you.

BLAKE7: I don't bargain with strangers who won't reveal their agendas.

WATCHER55: You will if you value your sister's life.

BLAKE7: Why are you threatening her? I'm asking you, please, leave her alone.

WATCHER55: I'm sorry, Blake. I don't think I want to leave her alone, and selfish people like me have tunnel vision when it comes to doing what we want. It's just the way we are, remember? You see, I think I'd like to hide in her room. In her closet, perhaps, the one with the three pairs of running shoes. I love those new Nike spikes she has. Maybe I could use them to shred that Paula Radcliffe poster that hangs on the wall opposite her closet. Then I could use them on Lorri herself!

BLAKE7: OK, you've made your point. You've been in our house. Heaven

help us, you've been in our house!
Listen to me—that's crossing the
line. That's a crime. This isn't a
game anymore. Enough, OK?
I'm going to have to involve the
police if you don't stop. Then the
game is up.

WATCHER55: My dear Blake: It never was a
game to me. Sure, I have had fun
along the way. But I'm not playing
games; I'm dead serious. You think
breaking and entering is a crime
to ME? I've done far, far worse.
Things that would make you retch
in horror. Things that would make
you scream. Things that WILL
make you scream.

BLAKE7: Please…

WATCHER55: Don't beg. It doesn't work. Now, listen to me. In a few moments, I will
end this session. At that time, go to
your mailbox. In it, you'll find a
sealed envelope. It contains
detailed directions on a few tasks
you are to complete tomorrow
night. It also contains a lock of
your sister's hair, just so you know
how close I've been to her—and

how close I can get again if you disobey me. She has very tiny ears under all that hair—did you know that? I thought about taking one of them. And don't bother to turn the envelope over to any authorities. Don't involve them at all. They'll find nothing, and then your sister's blood will flow like a fountain.

BLAKE7: Please, why are you doing this? What have you got against my sister?

WATCHER55: Your sister? She's a punk. She means nothing to us. She's just a pawn. It's you we want; it's always been you. Messing with your scrawny sister and your pathetic friends, that was just a bonus. My superiors let me do that just for kicks. The seeds of doubt I've sown in their troubled minds, the nightmares I've given them, the growing sense of paranoia? It's all just garnish around the main course. The Christian pig with a rotted apple in its holy mouth—you.

BLAKE7: I don't understand…what do you want from me? I have tried to help you, Haddon. I even defended you when my friends started to ridicule you.

WATCHER55: Shut up! No one ridicules me. You are not to say any more to me, unless it's a direct answer to one of my questions. Do not test me again. Just because your sister isn't my target, don't think I won't destroy her if that's what it takes to secure your cooperation, understand?

BLAKE7: Yes, sir.

WATCHER55: Good. Now, go get the letter. Read it. Obey it. Especially the part about running to your two destinations tomorrow. You are not to drive. You are not to share the letter's contents with anyone. We will be talking again in less than twenty-four hours—you from a location indicated in the letter. I am graciously giving you some time to get your affairs in order. Use the time well, Blake. They constitute your final hours on earth. I must repeat—do not disobey anything! Or your sister will experience a slow, terrible, degrading, and unfathomably painful death. Do you understand me?

BLAKE7: Yes.

WATCHER55: Good. Sweet dreams, Blake. Nice job on the debate. You won, and that earned me a humiliating punishment. But tomorrow, I'll feel much better. You, on the other hand… Well, good night, my friend. Good, last night.

Private Chat #132

Good-bye, Blake

PARTICIPANTS HERE: 5
Blake7 • Watcher55 • JennSmiles • Strider77 • CrossKrys

CROSSKRYS: Hey, what's with the "Good-bye, Blake" header? You goin' somewhere, B?

BLAKE7: The header wasn't my idea, Krys. But I am going somewhere.

STRIDER77: Blake, where ARE you?

JENNSMILES: Wait a minute, Stride. You mean Blake's not at home with you?

STRIDER77: No, he took off running a while ago. And, Blake, I hate you for kissing me on the forehead like that and looking at me with those puppy-dog eyes. I don't want your stinkin' pity, got it?

Blake7: It wasn't pity, Lorri. It was love. You'll understand soon enough. I sent you an email, which you'll get in about an hour. There's also one for Mom and Dad. You'll get one as well, Jenn and Krys.

JennSmiles: OK, I'm hating the sound of this. What's up, B?

Watcher55: Perhaps I can explain. You see, girls, Blake is going away. Forever.

CrossKrys: Blake, is that true? Where are you going? Or does he mean…?

Blake7: I am afraid so, Krys. I have no choice.

JennSmiles: Yes, you do. Listen, freak, this has gone too far. I'm calling the police. I'll call the FBI if I have to.

Watcher55: Go ahead. They won't find me. And even if they did, well, this was just one big role-play.

JennSmiles: They won't believe that.

WATCHER55: Sure they will. After all, one of YOU invited me to play....

JENNSMILES: Excuse me, but you put the UN in uninvited. Nobody invited you to this party. You crashed it, remember?

WATCHER55: Perhaps you should type your obnoxious "wrong answer" sound now, Jennifer. Shouldn't she, Ghost?

STRIDER77: I'm afraid so.

JENNSMILES: Stride, why is he calling you "Ghost"?

STRIDER7: It's kind of a code name.

CROSSKRYS: OK, I'm supposed to be Ms. Honor Student, but I'm lost here. What's going on?

STRIDER77: Blake, I'm sorry. I just wanted to teach you a lesson. Put you in your place. Pay you back for making me live in your shadow all of my stinkin' life. Subjecting me to all the expectations and pressure. You're just so freakin' holy-perfect all the time. You make me sick! But things kinda got outta hand.

BLAKE7: I'm sorry, Lorri, for what I put you through. I didn't mean to; I promise. I was just trying too hard. Jenn helped me see that. I was more concerned with setting a perfect example for you than I was with being your brother, your friend. And I never let you see the human side of me. The side that's scared, worried, lonely. The side that doubts, that cries. I was wrong, Lorri. Please forgive me.

WATCHER55: OK, enough! This is starting to sound like one of those nause-ating after-school specials. Blake, QUICKLY say your final good-byes and run to the appointed place to await your fate.

STRIDER77: Time out, Haddon. He doesn't have to go anywhere. Look, you've made your point. You did all I wanted and more. You've taught him a lesson he'll never forget. Now it's time to back off and col-lect your reward. Let's not go over-board with the "await your fate" crap. I don't like the sound of that.

WATCHER55: You're giving ME orders? Ha! You are truly a childish fool, Ghost. You think I accomplished so much just for a public meeting with you? You think you're worth all that? You're crazy. You're delusional. You're a supposed prodigy; you know what delusional means, don't you? And let's get something straight here: I'm done hearing your demands. You have no choice. Neither does Blake.

STRIDER77: What do you mean? Blake doesn't have to do anything you say.

WATCHER55: Actually, he does. That is, if he wants you to live to see your fourteenth birthday. Too bad it won't be a "Sweet Fourteen." Too bad you're already, how shall we put it…damaged goods.

STRIDER77: I'm not damaged, Botcher. At least not the way you're thinking. Who's the fool now, huh?

WATCHER55: If you betrayed me…

STRIDER77: No "ifs" about it. You got punked. Just how stupid do you think I am?

Blake7: Lorri, you mean nothing happened at the party?

Strider77: Well, almost nothing. I've heard about a few things that have happened at Greg's parties. It's Roofies Central over there. So when Tom brought Bri and me these big red cups of beer, I got suspicious. So when his back was turned, Bri and I dumped our brews on the carpet.

JennSmiles: Gosh, I sure hope Greg's parents use Scotchgard!

Watcher55: Silence! Ghost, you will pay! I hate you, you little she-pig!

Blake7: Lorri, I love you.

JennSmiles: I love ya too, Stride!

CrossKrys: Sign me up for the Lorri Love Train as well!

Strider77: Thanks, guys. See, Blake, I'm not just a dumb kid. And I want to finish the story: So after we dump the beers, Bri and I start acting all dizzy and stuff. And what does good old Tom do? He says he'll take us to a room so we can lie down. He says there has been a flu bug going around. Ain't he a sweetie? So we lie down on these twin beds, and Tom leaves the room for a few. When he comes back, we both jump up and start screaming at him. The phrase "statutory rape" was uttered a few times. Along with a few others I won't repeat. You might get upset, Blake. Bri also spoke of her big brothers and their collection of power tools.

WATCHER55: You little liar!

STRIDER77: Oh, ouch, Watcher. Comin' from a lyin' sack like you, that cuts like a knife! Now, as I said before, deal's off. Leave us alone. What I did was a mistake. I never should have hooked up with you in the first place. So take the nearest exit out of our lives, forever.

JENNSMILES: Yeah, go haunt an amusement park or something.

WATCHER55: I don't think that will be necessary. I hope you've had a good time with your teen-time banter, because you're about to experience some real, grown-up TERROR. But to show my magnanimity, I will release you from our deal, Lorri. However, there is another deal that will stand. And that is my pact with you, Blake. That pact is still in effect, isn't it, Blake?

BLAKE7: Yes.

STRIDER77: No way! Blake, you don't have to do anything this loser says!

BLAKE7: I'm afraid I do. He'll hurt you if I don't.

JENNSMILES: But, B, what makes you think he won't do…whatever to you, then come after Lorri anyway?

WATCHER55: I can answer that for you, Jennifer. Blake knows his sister will be safe, because after the authorities find his body, they'll take this whole matter quite seriously. They'll protect Lorri from me. In fact, they'll probably recommend a change of location, maybe of identity as well. So I'm sorry, Jenn and Krys, but it appears you'll be losing your little friend. And your big Blake-friend as well, of course.

JennSmiles: I hate you! You are pure evil!

Watcher55: You noticed that, eh? Thanks for the compliment. Oh, and I realize that I must amend something I said in my last statement: I spoke of the authorities finding Blake's body. I didn't mean that.

JennSmiles: Thank goodness!

Watcher55: I meant body PARTS! And with that, it's time to run to "our spot," Blake. Our secret spot. Run fast. Don't keep me waiting.

Blake7: OK.

Strider77: Blakey, NO!!!!!!!!!!!!!!!!!!!!!!!!!!!

Watcher55: BLAKEY? Oh, I'm gonna retch!

Strider77: Just leave him alone, OK? Leave my brother alone!

WATCHER55: He's not your brother anymore. He's not your anything. He's mine, body and soul!

JOSHUA: You don't speak the truth.

WATCHER55: Huh? Who are you? Is this you, Krys? I have noticed you have been silent for a while. Is this a pathetic attempt to save your friend? It won't work. Come on, confess, Krys. "Joshua" is you. Or is he one of your pathetic friends?

JOSHUA: I am Krys's friend. Pathetic? You will see.

WATCHER55: You are a friend of Krys, eh? I didn't know she had any friends beyond this pack of vermin. So what shall I call you? Is Joshua your real name?

JOSHUA: It is one of my real names. But if you prefer, you may call me KING OF KINGS, LORD OF LORDS, THE SON OF THE MOST HIGH, THE ALPHA AND THE OMEGA.

JENNSMILES: Oh, sweet Jesus!

Joshua: That works for me as well.

Watcher55: I'm not buying this. Your words don't frighten me. Do you know who I am?

Joshua: I do. Do you know who I AM?

Watcher55: Oh, sure! You're the son of God. Right! Oh my! The son of God is confronting me! Whatever shall I do?

Joshua: You have two choices. Flee…or bow down!

JennSmiles: Hey, he left! Without even a parting shot. I never thought he'd let anybody get the last word on him.

Blake7: Is he really gone?

Joshua: Yes.

JennSmiles: Are you really, uh…?

Joshua: What do you think?

JennSmiles: I think we should thank you.

Blake7: Yes, thank you!

Joshua: You are welcome.

JennSmiles: So we did some cyber-talking with your DAD a while ago. He's wonderful.

Joshua: Yes, He is.

JennSmiles: And, you know, I talk to you guys all the time now.

Joshua: Yes, we know.

JennSmiles: Sorry about all the yelling sometimes.

Joshua: You are in good company. David was a yeller. Job too.

JennSmiles: So it's OK to keep telling you how I feel—no matter what those feelings are?

Joshua: Yes. David and Job did. Much of what they said is in the Bible.

JennSmiles: Well, right now I want to tell you that I'm still scared, I must admit.

I mean, Watcher sure set a new world record for Freestyle Fleeing when you showed up, but he's still dangerous. I'm scared for Blake. I'm scared for Lorri. It seems like this guy is near them.

BLAKE7: He is. He put a letter in our mail-box. And I'm pretty sure he's been in our house.

JENNSMILES: Oh no! OK, this is some trippy stuff here! Lord, please keep my friends safe. Please!

JOSHUA: None of you needs to fear.

STRIDER77: Well, that's easy for you to say, whoever you are.

JENNSMILES: I have to kinda agree with Lorri here, Sir. I mean, I don't think any of us would be so afraid if you could send an army of angels or something to the Randall house.

JOSHUA: Lorri, get up from your computer. Go and look out a window. Come back and tell us what you see.

STRIDER77: OK. I'll be back in a couple minutes. But I doubt I'm gonna see anything that's gonna rock my world. Talk to you all in a few.

Private Chat #132

Good-bye, Blake, Version 2.0

 PARTICIPANTS HERE: 5
JennSmiles • CrossKrys• Strider77 • Blake7 • Joshua

STRIDER77: OK, Joshua, you must be an angel or a wizard or something. Consider my world officially rocked!

BLAKE7: What's up, Lor? Are there really angels outside our house?

STRIDER77: Not unless angels are wearing sweats, jeans, and WWJD T-shirts these days.

JENNSMILES: ?

STRIDER77: Blake, Jenn, everyone...the front yard is FULL of people. They're lining the sidewalk, even. The backyard's packed too.

BLAKE7: Who is "they," Lorri? WHO?

STRIDER77: It's people from our church—your church...whatever. I mean, the whole church softball team is out there—with their bats!

JENNSMILES: Oh, thank the Lord!

JOSHUA: You are welcome.

STRIDER77: And, B, I know I don't go to church that much anymore, so I'm not the best authority, but I don't think all of these people are from Covenant. The Daltons—aren't they Catholic? And the Taylors—I'm pretty sure they are Methodists.

BLAKE7: It sounds like people from other denominations have our back, Lorri.

JENNSMILES: How did you pull that one off, Sir? Interdenominational unity? That's TRULY a miracle.

JOSHUA: In my eyes, there are no denomi-nations.

BLAKE7: Amen to that. Thank you so much, Lord. I am so grateful to you. But

I'm also a bit confused. How did all these people hear about what was going on? How did they respond so quickly?

JOSHUA: Prayer chains are for more than spreading gossip, Blake. When Lorri slipped from the computer to tell your parents what was going on, they went to the phones immediately. And Krys reached out to many from her computer. Prayers rose to me from many homes, many churches, even some unexpected sources.

CROSSKRYS: And I notified the people at our ISP. They say they can track down Watcher. They'll find him, Lorri.

STRIDER77: If the police don't find him first. Sergeant Baker still goes to our church, doesn't he, Blake?

BLAKE7: Yeah. And he's not the only one from the law. There's this new guy, Pat, who rides to church every Sunday on his mountain bike.

JENNSMILES: That is cool! Man, will wonders never cease?

BLAKE7: I doubt it. We serve a God of wonders.

JOSHUA: Yes, you do.

STRIDER77: Hey, I need to say something here. I am sorry. To all of you. Especially you, Blake. Don't get me wrong— we're gonna have to deal with some stuff. And I still don't know how I feel about this whole faith thing. But you put your life on the line for me. You got guts. I'll never forget how you put yourself out there for me. Thanks.

BLAKE7: Lorri, you're my sister. I'd go to war for you. And thanks for saying I have guts, but what I really have is Joshua's example, Jesus' example. He gets all the credit. He gave me courage. When I agreed to run to the top of the Bluff to meet Watcher, I thought I was going to melt, the fear was so hot. But I prayed, and the Lord gave me the strength to do what I had to do.

STRIDER77: Well, what you have to do now is come home. I want you here. I need you here. Where are you, anyway?

BLAKE7: I'm at the library, using one of their computers. But I'm on my way now. It's a ten-minute run from here to home. I'll be there in five.

JENNSMILES: Godspeed, my friend.

JOSHUA: He can be assured of that.

CROSSKRYS: Lord, thank you for saving my friends. Thanks for hearing my prayers.

JOSHUA: I always do. I must go now, my friends. You know where to find me. And keep reading the red letters.

STRIDER77: Huh?

JENNSMILES: Stride, your bro sent Krys and me Bibles that have all of Jesus' words in red. We've made a pact that we'll "Read the Red" every day.

CROSSKRYS: Red has become my favorite color.

JOSHUA: ☺

CROSSKRYS: Lord, thank you again for intervening tonight. BTW, this has got me thinking, and I have to ask, when are you doing the Big Comeback? You know, the white horse, the trumpet blast, the triumphant return?

JOSHUA: I can't say.

JENNSMILES: Huh? YOU can't? For real?

JOSHUA: Jennifer, next time you are in the red letters, read Matthew 24:36. There I say, "No one knows about that day or hour, not even the angels in heaven, nor the Son, but only the Father." If I didn't know this information when I walked the earth, what makes you think I'll tell you now?

CROSSKRYS: But if you didn't know, why are people here so obsessed with trying so hard to predict when you'll be back? At my church, they have charts and graphs galore. Are you saying that's all a waste of time?

JOSHUA: I am saying, "Be ready." There is nothing wrong with being watchful, being prepared. But my greatest commandment is not "Try to predict the day and hour of my return." My greatest commandment is "Love the Lord your God with all your heart, mind, soul, and strength. And the second is like it: Love your neighbor as yourself." Those are the commandments that should be the root and foundation of your lives.

STRIDER77: Speaking of love, Blake's home. I hear his voice. He's calling me! I gotta go see him.

JENNSMILES: Rock on, Stride. Hug your bro for me.

CROSSKRYS: For me too.

JOSHUA: For me too.

STRIDER77: Will do. Jenn, Krys, will you forgive me?

JENNSMILES: Consider it done. I'm just glad you are safe.

CrossKrys: Lorri, I have been forgiven for so much—it's only natural that I forgive you.

Strider77: Thanks, women. As for you, Joshua, I'm not sure you're really the son of God—especially since I'm not even sure there is a God. But I feel this goodness that's, like, radiating from your words. And I know you have power, somehow. I don't know how you smoked Watcher, but I thank you. Thank you for saving my brother.

Joshua: You are welcome.

Strider77: I can't lie and say I'm going to go and get into a whole religion thing with you, but I won't forget what you did tonight. Ever.

Joshua: I am not interested in a "religion thing" with you either, Lorri. I want a relationship with you.

Strider77: Really?

Joshua: Really.

STRIDER77: I will think on that, I promise. And if I want to talk with you, can I find you here?

JOSHUA: You will always be able to find me. You don't need a computer. You don't need a church building. You don't need a Christian vocabulary. Just call out to me, and I will be there for you.

STRIDER77: But where exactly is "there"? I don't understand it. Like, you are communicating with us on our computers, you were hearing Krys's prayers, you're in the red letters.... Did I miss any place?

JOSHUA: Yes, including one very important place.

STRIDER77: And where is that?

JOSHUA: At the door of your heart, knocking.

STRIDER77: Yeah? You know, I think I can feel that. I'm sorry that I haven't answered, but that doesn't mean I'm not home, OK? Please keep knocking.

JOSHUA: I will.

STRIDER77: Oh my! Blake's here, standing in the doorway! He's all sweaty, but it's a beautiful sight. Time to deliver those hugs! I'm out, y'all.

Private Chat #133

The Morning After

PEOPLE HERE: 3
Blake7 • CrossKrys • JennSmiles

JENNSMILES: So, B, you have any company last night? LOL!

BLAKE7: Yeah, it was something. There were people from just about every church in town. Dad had to make three trips to the grocery store. Anybody who has stock in coffee and Pepperidge Farms cookies is rich today.

CROSSKRYS: That is off the chain! How long did everyone stay? Did you pull an all-nighter?

BLAKE7: Most just hung until the police showed up with the news about Haddon. But a few, including the softball team, stuck around just in case.

JennSmiles: News about Haddon? Spill it!

Blake7: They found him. He has an apartment not far from here. His last name is Shadonna—that's where he got the Haddon moniker. The police say they found "disturbing materials" at his place. I heard one officer say something about guns, martial arts weapons, and a vast collection of kiddie porn. And apparently Lorri and I haven't been his only targets. He's been trying to lure girls Lorri's age into meeting him. He's been the subject of a sting. I think they were close to catching him.

JennSmiles: How old is he?

Blake7: I don't know for sure. I think the police said about mid-thirties.

JennSmiles: And he's macking on little girls? What a perv!

CrossKrys: But what about you, B? You're not a little girl. Why was he so obsessed with you? How did he even know about you?

BLAKE7: They're not sure about that. But I think it has something to do with my being a Christian. Lorri says she met him in some random chat room early this summer. They got to be friends, and eventually she started sharing her resentment toward me. I think that's where he saw his opening. Then she started secretly inviting him into chats with us. I know that she just wanted to put me in my place, but Watcher had other plans all along. He lived close by, so he probably shadowed us. That's probably how he got her "e-dentity" in the first place.

CROSSKRYS: But why did you get on his radar? I mean, I know that Southern Cali's a wild place, but you're not the only Christian there.

JENNSMILES: Yeah, but a guy like Blake can really do damage to the "other side." Know what I mean?

BLAKE7: Thanks, Jenn. And I have to admit, I'm shaken. But I'm going to keep bringin' the damage. I won't be quiet about Jesus. I won't quit spreading the truth. The gates of hell aren't going to prevail against us. We're kicking them down. But we have to be smart. We have to put on God's armor, like it says in Ephesians.

CrossKrys: Hey, B, is Lorri with you? I'd like to talk to her, see how she's doing.

Blake7: Nah, she's not here. She's still asleep. She's whipped.

JennSmiles: Do you think she's seen the light?

Blake7: Yeah, I think she's glimpsed it. Now we just have to hope she will step outside her cold shell and bask in its warmth.

JennSmiles: Hope and pray, you mean.

CrossKrys: Speaking of prayer, what do you suppose Joshua meant when He spoke of prayer from "unexpected sources"?

Blake7: I'm inviting someone in who I think can explain that. I got an email from him earlier this morning. And we've been trading IMs for the past few minutes.

A.C.008: Yo, what's poppin'?

JennSmiles: Ace, is that you?

A.C.008: As far as I know.

JennSmiles: YOU are the unexpected prayer source? Get out!

A.C.008: Well, don't get the wrong idea. I'm not like you guys. But here in the, uh, treatment facility where I am now, they talk about a Higher Power. I'm not sayin' it's God, necessarily. But last night I got this weird feeling, and I thought about Blake. And trust me, he is not in my thoughts very often. But I was like, "Yo, HP, I think my homeboy needs help, so do what you do."

JennSmiles: Ace, you're a rock star! And I'm so glad you're getting help. Maybe you can get level, for good.

A.C.008: I don't know, Jenn. I don't know if I can do it. I just know that today has been a pretty good day, so far. Hey, I gotta go. Time to pee in a cup. Keep emailing me, guys. Sometimes I even read them.

BLAKE7: We will keep the emails flying, Ace. And the prayers too.

A.C.008: I got no objections to that. I guess I could use a prayer or two.

CROSSKRYS: Good-bye, Ace.

JENNSMILES: Good-bye, my friend.

CROSSKRYS: Blake, do you think he's gonna make it?

BLAKE7: I don't know. He told me that some days he doesn't have much hope. But he's trying.

JENNSMILES: I don't like the way he disappears from our lives for so long, then just pops up. Every time I say good-bye, I wonder if it's the FINAL good-bye.

BLAKE7: I know. But let's keep praying and hoping. And let's keep sending emails to Ace. You heard him— sometimes he even reads them!

JENNSMILES: Yeah, we have to make sure we follow up.

BLAKE7: On that subject, I want to follow up on last night. How long did Joshua chat with you two last night? What did you talk about after I left, after Lorri left?

JENNSMILES: He didn't stay long after you showed up in the doorway.

CROSSKRYS: Yeah, He just told us that He loves us. And He told us to love each other. And He said He would be with us always, even to the end of the world.

JENNSMILES: He did ask us to deliver a message to you, Blake.

BLAKE7: Really?

JENNSMILES: Yeah, I just hope I can remember it....

BLAKE7: Come on, Jenn! Don't leave me hanging....

JENNSMILES: OK, B, here goes: "Well done, good and faithful servant."

BLAKE7: Whoa! I don't know what to say. I'm humbled.

JENNSMILES: It's not about what you say, B. It's about what you were willing to do. I wish I had a brother like you. You are bank!

CROSSKRYS: I'm glad we have a friend like you. And like Him too!

JENNSMILES: Amen to that.

BLAKE7: Krys, Jenn, thank you. I thank God I met both of you. I wish we all lived closer.

CROSSKRYS: Ah, but, Blake, close isn't about geography. We're close. I have a feeling we always will be.

JENNSMILES: Well said, Krys. You'd think you were a genius or something. Oh yeah, I forgot: You are!

CROSSKRYS: Oh please…

BLAKE7: Hey, I hate to break up the love-in, but I am *worked*. I think I got about twenty minutes of sleep—sitting up against Lorri's door. I gotta crash.

JENNSMILES: We understand, B. Go, rest. Sleep in peace. We'll talk later.

CROSSKRYS: I'm with Jenn. But before you go, we'd like to do something for you.

BLAKE7: For me? What is it?

CROSSKRYS: Well, there was a time a few months ago, when we were all kinda saying good-bye for the summer, that you pronounced a blessing on us. Now Jenn and I would like to return the favor. Consider it a welcome-home blessing.

BLAKE7: Thank you. That means so much to me. But don't do that blessing just for me. Do it for God's people everywhere. Everyone committed to fighting evil and embracing good. Everyone like Ace and Lorri, who are struggling to find the truth, sometimes even in spite of themselves.

CROSSKRYS: OK, B, it's a pact. So here goes, for you and everyone...

JennSmiles: Now may the Lord bless you and keep you…

CrossKrys: …and make His face to shine upon you…

JennSmiles: …and be gracious to you…

CrossKrys: …and turn His face toward you…

JennSmiles: …and give you peace.

Blake7: Amen to that.

EPILOGUE

Private Chat #134

The University of Now What?

PARTICIPANTS HERE: 2
JennSmiles • Strider77

JENNSMILES: Whoa, it's been a long time since it was just the two of us.

STRIDER77: Yeah. Just think of all that happened in the meanwhile. It's enough to blow ya mind.

JENNSMILES: Yeah, but I'll bet you'll ace your "How I Spent My Summer Vacation" essay assignment when school starts again.

STRIDER77: Thanks so much for bringing up school! I was trying to ENJOY the final few days of my summer freedom.

JennSmiles: Well, this summer you enjoyed your freedom a little too much.

Strider77: I know, I know. Believe me, there is no cautionary tale you can tell that I haven't already heard from Blake. But now he always asks permission before he lectures me—so I guess that's an improvement. And…

JennSmiles: And?

Strider77: <sigh> And I'm glad that he cares so much. Trust me, I'm not gonna forget that my brother was willing to take a bullet—probably even worse—for me. It's weird....

JennSmiles: What's weird?

Strider77: Well, I always thought my friends were so cool and that Blake was such a helpless Herb. But you know, a lot of my peeps were at that party, and they watched Tom drag me toward a bedroom to take advantage of me. And they didn't lift a finger to help me. I saw their faces, through my feigned haze, and some of them were even laughing. Laughing! I guess I found out who really cares about me.

JennSmiles: I'm glad.

Strider77: You should be. I'd include you in that caring group.

JennSmiles: For real?

Strider77: For real. I was thinking of you when Tom was leading me away. I was thinking how you wouldn't have sat there laughing.

JennSmiles: You got that right, woman. If I'd been there, Tom and his booty-hound posse would be singing soprano today.

Strider77: I know. I believe you.

JennSmiles: So I get to keep being your friend?

Strider77: Yeah. I could use a real friend. The crowd I used to roll with...they were users.

JennSmiles: I had some friends like that. They were like ticks that attached themselves to me and were getting fat off of my lifeblood.

STRIDER77: Yeah, exactly! Besides, something hit me at that party at Greg's. I went in there with a sense of purpose, so I guess I didn't get all caught up in the buzz of it. I was, like, seeing it through different eyes.

JENNSMILES: And?

STRIDER77: And I saw a bunch of people trying so hard to have a good time but not really succeeding.

JENNSMILES: Stride, there's hope for you yet. I'm totally feelin' what you're saying.

STRIDER77: Well, that's good, I guess. I don't know that we'll ever have EVERY-THING in common, but you are a true friend. Not like others. Blake has this poster in his room. It's a Nigerian proverb that goes, "Hold on to a true friend with both hands." So that's what I'm going to do.

JENNSMILES: I'm glad, Stride. But even if you let go, I'm not turning loose of you. Neither will God.

STRIDER77: I don't know how I feel about that. I don't even know if I believe it. But I know you pray for me—still, right?

JENNSMILES: Every day. Every night. Even at dusk.

STRIDER77: Don't stop, OK?

JENNSMILES: OK, who are you and what have you done with Lorri?

STRIDER77: It's no joke, Jenn. I'll take all the prayer I can get. It sure saved my bacon this summer. Besides…

JENNSMILES: Besides…what?

STRIDER77: Well, you were right about something. I guess I do have a soul itch. I don't know whether to thank you or curse you for that, but there you go. It is what it is.

JENNSMILES: If you think I'm crying now because you just kicked me in the heart, you're crazy. I'm a woman of steel, you know that.

STRIDER77: And if you think I'm biting the insides of my cheeks right now so that I WON'T cry, you're even crazier.

JENNSMILES: It's a good thing we're so tough.

STRIDER77: I know. I hate that "Tonight, on a very special *Touched by an Angel…*" crap.

JENNSMILES: Me too.

STRIDER77: So I'm gonna go run eight miles now. So why don't you go pray for me?

JENNSMILES: I will. And, Stride? When you're out there, under the sky that God made, breathing the air He provides, consider saying thank you. Thank you for life.

STRIDER77: I just might. But I know one thanks I have to say for sure. Thanks, Jenn. Thanks for not giving up on me. Thanks for never talking down to me. Thanks for defending me to my brother, who I know you respect—and who-you-have-a-crush-on-too-but-won't-admit-it.

JennSmiles: Just had to throw that in, didn't you? Had to get in a parting shot?

Strider77: Nah, that was just a joke. Here's my real parting shot. Jennifer, I have a feeling that maybe there is a God, because you're like an angel on earth. And you've touched my life.

JennSmiles: Wait—I thought you didn't believe in that *Touched by an Angel* crap.

Strider77: Well, I guess I lied.

JennSmiles: For once, I'm glad to hear that. Vaya con Dios.

Strider77: Thanks. I know what that means.

JennSmiles: I hope so. Dear God, I hope so.

Glossary of Internet Terms and Teen Vernacular

A/S/L = Age/Sex/Location. One of the first bits of information shared by Internet chatters.

Amped = Excited, enthusiastic (e.g., "I am so amped about having cocktail weenies for dinner tonight!").

Baked (or budded) = Under the influence of marijuana.

Bank = Something or someone who is trustworthy and reliable. As in "You are bank!"

Big ups (to you) = A term of commendation or compliment (e.g., "Big ups to you for giving me a Hummer for my birthday!").

Blunt = To put it bluntly, a blunt is a cigarette containing marijuana.

Booty hound = Someone preoccupied with the search for sex.

BRB = Short for "Be right back."

BTW = Short for "By the way."

Foo = Short for "fool." Can be used as a term of endearment, as in "Nice reverse lay-up, foo!" or derision, as in "Don't try to sell me any of that cheap aluminum siding, foo!"

Gat = Street slang for a handgun.

Ghetto (adjective) = Characteristic of a rough, street-wise, and criminal lifestyle (e.g., "That hip-hop artist is trying to look very ghetto, but he's actually a rich guy from Carmel.")

(To) Google = To seek information on someone or something using the Internet tool *Google.com*.

(To) Go PBS = To speak in academic, multisyllabic jargon.

Herb (pronounced with a hard H) = The twenty-first-century equivalent of a nerd.

IM = Instant Message. Internet chat participants can converse one-on-one via message boxes. Once a message is typed on the screen and sent, it appears instantaneously on the addressee's computer screen.

ISP = Short for Internet Service Provider.

J/K = Just kidding.

(To) Jones / Jonesin' = To crave something, as in "I've just hiked twenty miles through the desert, and now I'm jonesin' for a glass of brisk iced tea."

LOL = Laughing out loud. This acronym is used to acknowledge a good joke or quip.

Mook = An insignificant, contemptible person. Also, a person characterized by raunchy language and a preoccupation with sex. (This term should not be confused with "Mookie," a moniker for several fine baseball players, such as Mookie Wilson.)

Off the chain = Something cool or desirable (a variation of "off the hook," "off the meat rack," etc.).

Peeps = Slang for one's friends, one's people. (Also, we think this is a name for those little marshmallow bird-shaped candies that come out every Easter, but those particular Peeps don't figure in this book. Maybe next time.)

Phat = Ultra-cool. For example, "That new dc Talk CD is phat!" (Note: Be aware of the confusion that can arise from telling your girlfriend, "Hey, those jeans make you look phat!")

Playa = One who plays the field, has many romantic partners, and avoids committed relationships.

Played = To be tricked or defeated (as in "You got played, playa!"). Synonymous with "schooled" or "punked."

POS = Short for "parent over shoulder." Teens use this term to ensure that they are conversing without parental supervision.

'Rents = Slang, short for parents, as in "Man, my 'rents are going to start charging me rent!"

Ripped = In great physical condition, with well-defined muscles. Synonymous with "cut."

Roll = A generic, often overused verb used to signify the beginning of any action or as a substitute for numerous verbs (Example 1: "I'm going to roll like this [wear this sweater vest].") (Example 2: Question—"Do you wan' go play a game of lawn darts?" Answer—"No, I don't roll like that.")

Roofies = Slang for date-rape drugs.

Tight = Very cool. For example, "Yo, those new tights are tight!"

What's the what? = What, pray tell, is the problem, the latest news, etc.?

Appendix A:
Online Profiles

Blake7

NAME: Blake7.

LOCATION: Lost Angeles, for now. Ultimate destination is a higher place.

MARITAL STATUS: Waiting (at least until I'm thirty) for the right girl.

HOBBIES: Youth group. H.S. hoops & track (Eagles rule!). Reading C. S. Lewis, Brennan Manning, Fred Buechner, etc., and, of course, the Bible! And did I mention youth group?

OCCUPATION: Student (of high school and of life).

LIFE PHILOSOPHY: "What does the Lord require of you? To act justly and to love mercy and to walk humbly with your God." Micah 6:8

User Profile

JennSmiles

NAME:	JennSmiles (and sometimes JennCries, but that's OK).
LOCATION:	Living a sometimes-rocky life in the Rockies.
MARITAL STATUS:	Future divorcée.
HOBBIES:	Survival. Figuring out life. Learning to pray.
OCCUPATION:	Recent high-school graduate. Now it's on to the University of Now What?
LIFE PHILOSOPHY:	Sing the first verse of "Amazing Grace," and you'll pretty much get the picture.

CrossKrys

NAME: CrossKrys, also known as Krystal, KrysCross, and various other monikers.

LOCATION: The wild, wild west.

MARITAL STATUS: I am sixteen. I don't live in the Deep South. You figure it out.

HOBBIES: Hanging with my friends. Chatting online, especially with my best cyber-bud, Jenn. (Love ya, J!) Listening to music, especially dc Talk, Third Day, Superchic[k], Nichole Nordeman, etc. (You guys are like new friends to me—thanks!)

OCCUPATION: Occupied.

LIFE PHILOSOPHY: I have decided to follow Jesus, but I'm keepin' my tattoos.

A.C.008

Name: A.C.008 / Ace / Space Ace / Ace Wasted / Hey You.

Location: Wherever.

Marital Status: Single 4 Life.

Hobbies: Yeah, right...

Occupation: Whatever's handy, as long as it's not minimum wage.

Life Philosophy: When I get one, I'll let you know.

Strider77

NAME: Strider77 (Lorri).

LOCATION: Under my big brother's shadow.

MARITAL STATUS: This is SO not applicable.

HOBBIES: Running faster every day.

OCCUPATION: Don't want to think about this.

LIFE PHILOSOPHY: Life is a blood sport. Only the strong survive.

Watcher55

NAME: Watcher55.

LOCATION: I'll never tell.

MARITAL STATUS: I don't acknowledge outdated institutions.

HOBBIES: Studying life.

OCCUPATION: Leading researcher in the field of human motivation and behavior.

LIFE PHILOSOPHY: Follow me for the adventure of your life.

Appendix B

THE FINAL THREE CHAPTERS OF *IN THE CHAT ROOM WITH GOD*

Private Chat #118

Fond Farewells

 PARTICIPANTS HERE: 3
JennSmiles • CrossKrys • Blake7

CROSSKRYS: I hate this.

JENNSMILES: I'll second that emotion. Blake, Krys, you freaks. Why are you doing this to me?

BLAKE7: I'm sorry, guys. I'm going to miss this. I'm going to miss you both.

JENNSMILES: Ditto that, B. You really going to be away from your 'puter for the whole summer though?

BLAKE7: Pretty much. I've always wanted to bike across the country. Now is the time. Then when I get back, there's this track camp up north. I don't want to get smoked at regionals like I did this season. I've got to bring my mile time way down if I want to run with the big dogs.

JENNSMILES: Well, I guess I can respect that. But, you, Krys, are you sure that you won't be online this summer?

CROSSKRYS: Doubtful, but not hopeless. I'm spending the summer in Montana with Biological Mom. She's an avowed technophobe. But I imagine I might make some friends who can hook me up. Don't be surprised if I pop up on your screen sometime.

JENNSMILES: Thank God for that.

CROSSKRYS: Speaking of the deity—I wonder why he's not chatting right now. Maybe he wants to give us some time.

JENNSMILES: Yeah. And speaking of missing persons, I have not heard a l'il peep from Ace in a long time. I got this long, rambling, incoherent e-mail a while back. He was still trying to justify using drugs and stuff, but his stance was rather feckless.

CROSSKRYS: Feckless? Nice word.

JENNSMILES: Yep. I'm still on that new-word-a-day thing. Pretty impressive, huh?

CROSSKRYS: Do you know what feckless means, exactly?

JENNSMILES: Sure…uh, it means that something lacks feck. Did I use it wrong?

CROSSKRYS: Nah, you're good.

JENNSMILES: Thanks. You're good too.

BLAKE7: Hey, girls, I'd like you to meet someone. Lorri (a.k.a. Strider77) is my little sister. She's going to keep my computer warm for me while I'm gone. She's been wanting to meet you, so I figured now is the time.

STRIDER77: Hey.

CROSSKRYS: Hey right back.

JennSmiles: It's a pleasure, Lorri. Blake, you never even told me you had a sister. It's weird; we've been friends the whole year, and you know everything about Krys and me. But we know very little about you.

Blake7: Maybe that will change when I return.

CrossKrys: It better. So, Lorri, how old are you?

Strider77: Thirteen. You?

CrossKrys: Sixteen.

JennSmiles: I'm eighteen, but I've been eighteen since I was thirteen, really.

Strider77: I've been thirteen since March 23.

JennSmiles: Well, it will be nice to have someone to keep me company, since all my other friends are DESERTING ME.

God: Not everyone is deserting you.

JennSmiles: You are here! Yes! I'd say, "Long time, no talk," but we've been talking almost every night lately.

GOD: Yes, we have.

BLAKE7: Jenn, I can't tell you how happy I am.

JENNSMILES: Well, don't get too happy, Blake-o. You don't hear what I say sometimes. I think God and I are going to have one of those stormy relationships. And stormy is a fitting word. Because that's what my life is. Parents fighting around me, guys hassling me, teachers pressuring me to go to college. Any chance of calming things down for me, God?

GOD: You carried your niece into your house last week because it was pouring outside. You wrapped your jacket around her and used your body to shield her from the storm.

JENNSMILES: Why do I get the impression that there's a lesson coming here?

GOD: You are right. If you could have seen your niece's face as she nestled close to you, you would have seen peace in her eyes. She knew that a storm was raging around her. But she was warm, safe, and dry in your arms. That's the way it is with Me. Sometimes I will calm the storms. But other times, I will let them rage and calm My children instead.

JENNSMILES: I used to have nothing to hold on to during life's, uh, storms. Now perhaps I do.

BLAKE7: What about you, Krys? What effect has this past year of chats had on you?

CROSSKRYS: You mean other than the fact that I've met friends I never want to lose? Or that I've spoken to God live and in person? Sometimes I wake up from a dead sleep and say to myself, "Oh, my, I've met God!" How cool is that? It's weird—I came up with my screen name because I am a big-time cross-country skier. But now the "cross" part has a different meaning to me.

JENNSMILES: Well, I hate to break up this little happy-fest, but the fact is that we are going somewhat separate ways now, and I'm going to miss my friends. God, will you chat online with me anymore, with us anymore?

GOD: I am always talking to My children.

JENNSMILES: What do you mean? I'm afraid of losing this. Of losing touch.

GOD: Blake, would you get your Bible for us? You left it on the TV.

BLAKE7: OK, BRB

Private Chat #118

Fond Farewells, Version 2.0

 PARTICIPANTS HERE: 5
Strider77 • Blake7 • God • CrossKrys • JennSmiles

BLAKE7: I'm back with Bible in hand.

GOD: Please read Isaiah 41:10. What do I say there?

BLAKE7: "Do not fear, for I am with you; do not be dismayed, for I am your God. I will strengthen you and help you; I will uphold you with my right-eous right hand."

JENNSMILES: But how will you do that? How can you be with me if I can't find you in a Private Chat anymore?

GOD: Watch and see. Those who seek Me find Me. Whether they have a computer is not relevant. I will never leave you. Remember that.

BLAKE7: Jenn, we have an entire Book that is God's ongoing message to us. We have pastors, artists, musicians, teachers. And David said that his own heart instructed him. So listen to God's messengers. And listen to your heart.

JENNSMILES: I will do that. Since I have been drawing closer to God, it's like my heart has been telling me some cool stuff. I don't feel so tossed around like a rag doll in a rottweiler's mouth anymore. But, still, what am I going to do without you guys? Without these times?

CROSSKRYS: Well, Jenn, my friend, we have talked about life over the past year. Maybe it's time to log off and start LIVING it.

GOD: An excellent idea, Krys. Life is worth living big. I want you to have life, and have it abundantly. I am not the Great Denier, as some have said. I am the Great Giver. I give you freedom. And I give you wisdom so that you may fully and purely enjoy that freedom, not abuse or squander it.

JennSmiles: This may sound dumb, but can we really be happy and not feel guilty about it? We don't have to be all dour and sour—or red-faced and pompous like some of those TV preachers?

God: Be happy, young friends. Let your hearts give you joy in the days of your youth. May you know always what your life is worth. This is your time. Drink life in. Breathe it in. Create something beautiful. Love someone unlovable. Say something bold and true. Give. Forgive. Sing. Revolutionize your world for good.

JennSmiles: I will try. But you've got my back, right, God?

God: I do. I will sustain you. You will experience trouble in this world. But take heart, I have overcome the world. Difficult people, difficult times, they are not your enemy. They are your opportunity! And remember, I am with you always. I am watching over you, with love and hope. I, My angels, and all the heroes of the faith. We cheer you on. My angels celebrated for all they were worth when I saw you from the road, heading for home.

JennSmiles: That is mad cool.

CrossKrys: So, God, is this really it for you and the chat rooms?

God: You will always be able to find Me. If not here, then somewhere else.

Blake7: Sir, would Jesus ever visit us in the chats, as You did?

God: All things are possible.

Blake7: …even finding the will to say good-bye to my friends. I have to get my bike to the shop for a tune-up. And the shop closes soon. Krys, Jenn, I will write to you whenever I can. I will think of you. I will pray for you. And let's all pray for Ace. We can't forget him. Anyway, thank you for inviting me into your world.

JENNSMILES: You better write, B. And maybe we can go to that church camp next summer, the one you e-mailed me about?

CROSSKRYS: Yeah, maybe we can all go. Well, I may have a 4.0, but I'm lousy at goodbyes. So I'll just say I love you all. And, Blake, I promise I'll try to find a church in Biological Mom's town. And if I charm my way into some computer-owning girl's life, you and I can carry on just like old times, Jenn. And we can get to know you, Blake's Little Sister.

STRIDER77: I'm looking forward to that.

JENNSMILES: OK, before we all get weepy, let's wrap this up. We've said what needs to be said. So, I'm gonna count to three, then we do the simultaneous log-off and shut-down, OK?

BLAKE7: OK, but I have a little benediction to pronounce as we go: Now may the Lord bless you and keep you…

JENNSMILES: One…

Blake7: …and make His face shine upon you and be gracious to you…

JennSmiles: Two…

Blake7: …and turn His face toward you and give you peace.

God: Amen.

JennSmiles: Three!

EPILOGUE

Private Chat #119

What Now?

PARTICIPANTS HERE: 2
Strider77 • JennSmiles

JENNSMILES: So, tell me, kid, are you anything like your brother?

STRIDER77: Well, not really. First, he's a guy, of course, and he's a lot faster than I am. But someday, I'm gonna smoke him like a Christmas ham.

JENNSMILES: Are you as much a person of faith as he is?

STRIDER77: Let's not go there. That's kind of a sore subject for me. See, our parents often FORCE me to go to church, and I hate it. But Blake goes because he wants to, so that makes me look really sorry by comparison. It's like Good Kid/Bad Kid. I'm tired of the unfavorable comparisons. I'm tired of living in his shadow. You know, sometimes I think of doing something really nasty just to show my parents how un-Blake-like I am.

JennSmiles: Do you believe in God, Lorri?

Strider77: You know, my parents don't even ask me that question. They just assume I do. And I don't know if I believe. I call myself a Christian, just like I call myself a Randall (that's our last name, in case you didn't know). It's like I inherited my name and my religion at birth. I never got a say in anything. I don't know. I guess I don't really believe God has much interest in someone like me. I'm just a kid with this bigger-than-life Super Brother whose goal is to save all of humanity. How do I deal with that? I'm just a confused kid who has no clue about life, to be honest.

JennSmiles: ☺

STRIDER77: You find all this funny?

JENNSMILES: No, not at all. It's just that I relate to you so much. And I'm just sitting here thinking, Whoa, do this girl and I have a LOT to talk about!

STRIDER77: OK, but don't think you're gonna flip me to being all religious like Blake. That's not who I am.

JENNSMILES: I won't try to flip you. But if it happens, it happens. I didn't think it would ever happen to me. But I flipped like a pancake. I heard this story about this father running down the road to love on his son… I need to tell you that story. I'm sure you've heard it before, but maybe you've never really heard it, know what I mean? I need to tell you lots of stuff. And I will listen to you too. I will do nothing but listen, if that's what you need on some particular day. Deal?

STRIDER77: That's cool with me. Do you think God or Jesus will join us sometime?

JENNSMILES: Maybe. But let's just become friends and see what happens. After what I've seen this past year, who knows whose name might pop up on the screen someday....

Acknowledgments

Our heartfelt, humble thanks to the following people...

Pastor Del Hafer (our dad) for biblical insight—and for challenging our minds, even when we were preteens, with the hard truths of Scripture and the daring writing of C. S. Lewis, R. C. Sproul, Francis Schaeffer, Charles Colson, and many others.

Brennan Manning and Steve Thurman for saying Grace.

Steve Taylor, Nichole Nordeman, dc Talk, Ashley Cleveland, Superchic[k], Jennifer Knapp, Sarah Masen, Sixpence None the Richer, Charlie Peacock, Third Day, Rich Mullins, Geoff Moore, and The Choir for songs that have revealed God's grace and truth and comforted us in days when hope was dim.

Chaplain Pat Cooperrider for showing a Christ-like heart to young people—and not so young people—every day.

Valerie Schroeder Skaret for showing us how a Christian young person can live purely in an impure world—and still be really cool.

Our siblings, Chadd and Bradd Hafer, for their friendship and brotherhood.

Natasha Sperling and everyone at Bethany House, we are grateful to be working with you!

Our wives (one for each of us), Jody and Lindsey Hafer, and our kids for believing in us, enduring deadline pressures and odd-hour writing binges, and letting us hog the family computers while researching and writing this book.

****

If you are a young person and this book connected with you, we recommend a syndicated radio program called ZJAM (check your local listings for broadcast times). Or log on to *www.ZJAM.com* and check out their live interactive chats, online Bible studies, and more. ZJAM presents relevant, cutting-edge music with a message—like Superchic[k]'s!

Especially if you find yourself lost, hurting, or struggling, please seek out their interactive *www.teenhopeline.com*, where you'll find wonderful people who will pray with you, talk with you, and do whatever they can to help you.

You can always contact us too, via *www.haferbros.com*.

Your friends,
Todd and Jedd

About the Authors

Jedd Hafer is a stand-up comic and youth speaker who works nationally. A finalist in the "Tonight Show with Jay Leno Comedy Challenge," he is also a two-time winner of the Colorado Young Writers award. A piece titled "Overheard at an Amy Grant Concert," which he wrote with his brother Todd, was chosen for the book *The Best Christian Writing 2000*. Jedd also works as a director at The Children's Ark, a home for troubled teens.

Todd Hafer is editorial director for Hallmark Inc.'s book and music divisions. He also tackles a variety of writing assignments for newspapers and magazines. He has won several national and international writing awards, a few of which his children haven't colored on or used to play army. *Stranger in the Chat Room* is his nineteenth book.

To learn more about the authors—or to send them an email—visit their Web site, *www.haferbros.com*.

VOLUME ONE

Learn about some of the biggest Jesus Freaks of all time: those who stood out from the crowd enough to be called martyrs. If Jesus was willing to give His life for me, and if these people, these martyrs, were willing to give up their lives for Him, how much does it take for me to truly dedicate my days on earth to Him?

Jesus Freaks by dcTalk and Voice of the Martyrs

INSPIRATION
REVOLUTION

VOLUME TWO

In this second volume, learn about those who stood against the culture of their day and made a difference. These individuals were not all martyrs, but they were all effective witnesses for Christ in societies that did not value the ways of Christ. These stories will not just inspire but challenge us with ideas of how we, too, can stand up against the culture of our day.

Jesus Freaks: Vol II by dcTalk

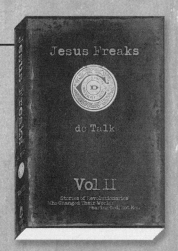

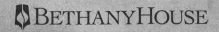
BETHANYHOUSE